Goodbye My Love, Goodbye...

A Novel by
CLIFTON LABREE

© 2004 by Author, Clifton LaBree

Published by
Fading Shadows Imprint
New Boston, New Hampshire, USA

ISBN-10: 1-943329-26-5
ISBN-13: 978-1-943329-26-7

Cover Design by Vivian LaBree

Dedicated to my wife Pauline, and my family, with thanks for all their support and encouragement

Chapter One

Late September 1955, in the small town of Wells, Maine.

The doorbell's loud ring woke Jon Burke from a sound sleep in the middle of the night. He turned on the light near the bedside stand and looked at his watch. It was two-thirty in the morning. Always concerned about phone calls or doorbells ringing in the middle of the night, his heart began to pound. They always meant bad news. He threw on a bathrobe and stumbled blindly toward the front door.

"Yes... yes, I'm coming," he cried, irritated by the loud bell. "Who's there?" he asked, still half asleep.

"This is Lieutenant Lear of the Maine State Police, Mr. Burke."

The authoritative voice gave him a chill. Could it be his wife, Jill, who was away on a consulting engineering project in upper state New York? Or was it pertaining to his son, Carl, at the University of New Hampshire in Durham, or his daughter, Ashley, living in Wells, Maine, with her husband Hal Perkins and Jon's brand new granddaughter, Nina, the joy of their lives? His mind was a nervous blank as he opened the door and asked, "What do you want at this ungodly hour in the morning?"

The young policeman held his hat in his left hand, gave Jon a hesitant look, and announced himself. "I'm Lieutenant Lear. Please, May I come in, Mr. Burke?"

"What's this all about, Lieutenant?" Jon asked, even more concerned by the somber look on the young policeman's face. He motioned for him to come into the living room.

"I'm the bearer of bad news, Mr. Burke. I'm assuming that you're Jon Burke."

"Yes, yes, continue, Lieutenant," he stammered.

1

"My headquarters just received a dispatch from New York. They believe that your wife, Jill Burke, was involved in a serious automobile accident. I'm here to confirm if she's at home, Sir?"

"No, she's an engineer and left for a project in New York and Pennsylvania yesterday…"

"According to the dispatch, they have her listed as Mrs. Jill Burke, 126 Forest Road, Wells, Maine."

"How serious is the accident, Officer?" Jon asked impatiently.

"It's my sad duty to inform you that she was instantly killed upon impact with a truck on a main highway near Glens Falls, NY." The policeman knew that he was shattering the man's world with the horrific news.

An inhuman cry pierced Jon's lips as he sought the support of a nearby chair. "Are you sure about your facts, Lieutenant?" He struggled to get the words out.

"Yes, Sir. I personally checked with the dispatcher from New York. I'm truly sorry, Mr. Burke. Is there anyone I can call to help you at this time? I'll be glad to call your minister or priest for some support. I'll stay with you for as long as needed. Do you want me to call your children or any other family member?"

Jon heard the policeman, but he was in a world of his own. "I… I don't understand. She left only two days ago and planned to return home within four days at the most. The bridge they were testing spanned the Delaware River at Port Jervis. She had called me once she arrived at the engineering field office…" He was completely unprepared to accept what the policeman had told him and still maintain rationality. The sickening news wiped out his ability to think straight. He gasped for breath and leaned his head back against the chair emitting convulsive sobs that worried the policeman.

All that he could do was place a comforting hand on Jon's shoulder and assure him that he was not alone. It was important that someone stay with the grieving person until they arrive at some level of reality. Lieutenant Lear felt sorry for the bereaved gentleman. He had just delivered the most terrorizing message a person can receive. The violent and sudden death of a loved one takes a while to completely register. The sudden rush of powerful emotions are difficult to control or predict.

2

Even in the midst of all the hurt and pain, Jon's mind was preparing him for the tasks ahead. He subconsciously thought of his daughter, Ashley, and son, Carl. How was he even going to inform them of the tragedy that had just struck? Sitting in the chair, he held his head in his two hands and wept until there were no more tears to flow.

The house was dark except for a light in the hallway coming from the bedroom. Lieutenant Lear looked for a light and turned on a lamp beside where Jon was sitting. He then placed a sheet of paper on the end table. "I'm going to leave you a copy of the dispatch we received from the New York State Police at Glens Falls, Mr. Burke. We do not have any more information than what is specified in the dispatch. There are numbers to call for further information. Their most pressing need is for positive identification of the body. We're quite positive that it's your wife. Are you prepared to go to New York to make that positive identification? I'm authorized to assist by transporting you there and back at your convenience. Do you understand me, Sir?"

Jon reached in his bathrobe for a handkerchief to blow his nose and wipe the tears from his eyes. "Your offer to help is appreciated, Lieutenant. Please do not contact my son or daughter until I've personally confirmed or denied identification. My God… I never dreamed that such a tragedy could visit our home. I was a soldier in World War Two and Korea and saw a lot of death, but this is personal, and for the first time in my life, I know how the deceased soldier's family members felt when confronted with deadly telegrams notifying the death of a loved one."

"I understand, Sir. I also served in Korea and the Second World War. If you need some time to yourself, I do understand. Can you be ready to travel soon?" Lieutenant Lear asked in a calm voice. The light was good enough that he could see several pictures of family members on a coffee table in front of the couch. He noted Jon was wearing a summer Army uniform with captain insignias on his lapel. His wife, Jill, was a petite blonde with a winning smile. He thought she was beautiful. Their daughter and son were still very young. It was a portrait of a happy family, and it made the young policeman sad that he had to be the messenger of death that ripped a permanent

3

tear in the family. He shrugged his shoulders and accepted the fact that it was a part of the job he had been trained to do after he got out of the Army.

"I'm prepared to get dressed and head out as soon as possible, Lieutenant. I'll drive myself to New York. You may notify the New York authorities that I'll be in Glens Falls by mid-morning. Thanks for the kind offer to chauffer me. May I keep this copy of the dispatch?"

"Yes, Sir. That's your copy. I'll call New York. I'm sorry I had to deliver such devastating news to you at this time in the morning. Goodbye. If you need any assistance in the future, please feel free to contact me. Here's my card." With that, Lieutenant Lear quietly exited the house. He notified New York dispatch that Jon Burke would soon be on his way to make positive identification.

Twenty minutes later, Jon backed his 1955 Studebaker pickup truck out of the garage, driving to the nearest service station to fill it with gas. The truck was good on the highway with the powerful 289 V/8 engine and overdrive transmission. He checked the tires, engine oil and washed the windshield. Once on the road, he had a tendency to set a steady pace to flow with the rest of the traffic. By mid-morning he was passing through Rutland, Vermont, then crossed into New York State. He stopped at Fort Ann to check his map. He was only miles from Glens Falls. He stopped at a construction site and asked directions from an officer directing traffic. Fifteen minutes later, he pulled into the parking lot of the police headquarters.

He walked inside to announce himself with a heavy heart, filled with anxiety. A middle-aged officer with glasses introduced himself to Jon. "I'm Captain Halloway, precinct commander. The Maine authorities alerted us that you were on your way. You made good time, Mister Burke. You have our sympathy."

"You're correct. This hasn't been an easy trip, Captain. Where did the accident take place?" Jon asked in a wavering voice.

Captain Halloway turned to him and replied, "It was a mile or so north of Glens Falls on Route 9. The vehicle she was in was traveling south on route 9 when it appeared that it veered into oncoming traffic. It was a massive head-on collision, Sir. Both parties were killed on impact. That's the truth as we know it. Please, follow me to the mortuary in the basement of the building. I caution you to be strong. In my opinion, the act you are about to perform is the most painful duty a person is ever called upon to do. If you need help, please let us assist you in getting through this ugly ordeal."

Jon prayed that the body in the drawer would not be Jill, his wife of several years. He knew that it defied logic, and it transferred the hurt onto some other person, but he was selfish enough to still pray that this ordeal pass him over. They were taken into a damp room with large lockers filling one whole wall. Several attendants stood by in case they were needed. Experience told them that most people need help before they can exit the room. An attendant pointed out a certain drawer to the Captain and backed away.

"Now, Mister Burke," Halloway whispered firmly with one hand on the drawer. "The first impact is the most traumatic. Just tell me if you need a little more time."

"Go ahead, Captain," Jon nodded. "Open the drawer."

Slowly, Captain Halloway began to pull the drawer out its full length, first exposing a pair of feet sticking out from a white sheet. Jon viewed them through a veil of tears. His knees were becoming unsteady. The corpse before him emitted an aroma of formaldehyde that violated his sense of smell. As the drawer continued to expose more of the corpse, he was looking into Jill's face! Her eyes were closed and the bluish pallor of the exposed skin slowly had the cold look of death. Her natural blonde hair was cut just below her ears. There was a black and blue bruise on her lower jaw. He had the feeling that if he spoke to her, she would answer him. All he had to do was wake her up, and everything would be all right. He touched her cold face and mumbled, "Why, Jill…why…Oh, dear God, why did you have to take her away from us at this time in our lives? The best years were ahead of us…Why?"

"Are you certain that this is your wife, Mister Burke?" asked Captain Halloway in a calm voice.

Jon was holding back a flood of tears. He felt weak and reached out to steady himself with the policeman's hand. "Yes… this is my wife, Jill." Turning from the dead figure, he gasped and cried out in a loud voice... "God, it hurts. Why now?"

Halloway and an attendant guided Jon back upstairs to the headquarters. "The Maine State Police informed me that you were an Army officer, Mister Burke, and that you would understand that we have a few documents that require your signature. All agencies associated with government business operate on paperwork. Police Departments are no different. We'll just be a few minutes, and you may leave. Can we get you anything, Sir? Your color is not very good."

"If you had a magic wand, you could remove the pain..."

"I understand. Please have a seat, and I'll make this as brief as possible," replied Captain Halloway.

"You mentioned paperwork, Captain. May I have a copy of the accident report and the coroner's autopsy report?"

"Of course. We also have your wife's clothing for you to take home."

"Where is the automobile now?"

"The vehicle is at a holding station at a garage just outside of town. It was a 1953 green Nash Ambassador," Captain Halloway mentioned.

"Was my wife driving that vehicle?" Jon asked. His head was filling with questions, searching for answers. "I don't recall the engineering firm having any such vehicle."

"Your wife was a passenger. The driver was Lauren Hopkins from Albany, New York. I'll personally see that you get a copy of every report pertaining to the accident. Sometimes it helps to know exactly what happened. Simple facts answering how, why, when and where, like the points in an Army field order, can sometimes help to ease the pain of not knowing," Captain Halloway said in a calm voice, placing a comforting hand on Jon's shoulder.

"You're right, Captain."

Jon felt as if he was in a separate world, oblivious to those around him. He searched his brain to make sure that he had asked all the right questions. Carl and Ashley both would demand knowing everything about the incident. He was always a methodical man and silently had been reconstructing the accident that took his wife and the mother of his children.

An hour later, he had copies of the reports he had asked for. The driver of the truck received no injuries from the impact. Jon planned on speaking to the driver when the time was right for them both. He also wanted to speak to the first officer who arrived at the scene. Patrolman Joseph Harvey happened to be first at the accident scene. He offered to take Jon out to the crash site on U.S. Route 9, north of Glens Falls in his Ford patrol car.

"Was my wife alive when you first arrived at the crash site?" Jon asked in a shaky voice.

"The severity of the accident impressed me, and my first concern was for the occupants of the car. The truck driver hollered to me from the cab of his truck that he was all right. He was shaken but not in need of emergency medical treatment. I first checked the man behind the steering wheel and had trouble opening the door. I was able to reach through the broken window to check for a pulse. He had a pulse at first and was bleeding profusely. Within a minute or two he had stopped breathing. I knew that the fire department was on its way, and they are better trained for emergency treatment of patients than I am. I then ran to the other side of the vehicle to your wife in the passenger compartment. She was slumped over the dashboard. She was already dead when I got to her, Mister Burke, I'm sorry. She did not have her seat belt on. The seat broke loose from its fastenings and drove her into the dash. I can honestly tell you that she died instantly. There was no evidence of anxiety or fear on her facial expression. People who die a painful death register the pain in some way. Your wife did not. I hope that's some comfort to you."

"It is, Officer. I appreciate your honesty."

The policeman pulled his patrol car off the road and turned on the flashing red lights. Instantly the traffic slowed ten miles an hour. "You can see the skid marks where the truck pushed the Nash backwards, dragging its wheels. The truck driver told me that the Nash simply darted into the northbound lane without notice almost as if it was intentional, which I doubt. It may have been one of those rare moments when the driver was not alert enough to detect his car's drift to the left. They were heading south on the western side of the road."

Jon studied the situation, visualizing the way the accident unfolded. He now possessed as much information as anybody.

It was important that he knew precisely how his wife died. The officer had been helpful in fulfilling that wish. He had been professional and thorough in carrying out his duties. Jon had locked the images in his heart and was ready to return to Glens Falls for his truck.

Suddenly a new Buick sedan pulled behind the patrol car and stopped. It was driven by a young man. A middle-aged woman leaped from the Buick and ran to confront the policeman. She was disheveled with red eyes and a gaunt stare on her contorted face.

"Is this where the accident took place?" she exclaimed breathlessly.

Patrolman Harvey reached out to calm her. "Who are you, Ma'am?"

"I'm Amber Hopkins, the wife of the man who was killed here. Captain Halloway told me that Patrolman Harvey would be at the site with the husband of the woman who was also in the crash."

Chapter Two

"Yes, Mister Burke is here with me. I've just described the scene as I found it when I first arrived. Are you all right, Ma'am?" he asked, concerned that she was so overwrought with grief.

"What do you think, Officer? Wouldn't any normal person be upset finding her husband was killed in an automobile accident with a total stranger?" she cried in a loud voice.

Her son, fighting his own grief, placed an arm about his mother. "Please excuse my mother. I'm her son, Alfred. We just came from the mortuary. It's been the most horrifying experience of our lives. Would you please describe the accident scene one more time, Officer? It will help us understand how things happened."

"It's my pleasure, Alfred. I really do understand your position, Mrs. Hopkins. You have my sincere sympathy." The officer then proceeded to describe the accident as he did to Jon.

Jon could relate to the hurt and anger that was consuming the woman. He did not know and had never heard of any such person as Lauren Hopkins associated with the Hastings Engineering firm in Philadelphia. Hastings had called upon his wife for various technical services throughout the eastern portion of the country and Canada. She was a brilliant design engineer and had specialized in metal fatigue. Throughout New England she had been responsible for the closing of several bridges due to failing support braces.

Earlier in the month she had received a call from Hastings to examine the main support girders on the bridge that spans the Delaware River at Port Jervis on the New York-Pennsylvania border. Port Jervis was a hundred and fifty miles from Glens Falls! That fact bothered him, yet he felt that there had to be some logical explanation. Perhaps she was checking other bridges. His mind was still trying to accept the fact that he had kissed his beloved Jill for the last time. He continued to question why? Why at this time in their lives?

Jon found it appropriate to remain in the police cruiser while the officer kindly went over the sequence of events at the crash site with Mrs. Hopkins and her son. Shortly they left the scene, and Patrolman Harvey returned to the cruiser, moved by the pain the accident had thrust upon everybody.

"I'll take you over to the compound where the Nash is stored. I estimate it was traveling at least fifty miles per hour headed south. The trucker told me he had been slowed down some by the slight upgrade of the road heading north. He estimated he was doing forty miles per hour. That gives an impact of ninety to one hundred miles per hour."

"My God," exclaimed Jon. "I would like to see the vehicle. How thoroughly did your people go over the Nash?"

"We essentially removed the bodies, Mister Burke. There was never any question of alcohol, drugs, or traffic violations. It was simply a tragic human error, an accident. The vehicle and its contents are still private property. The Nash was registered in Lauren Hopkin's name."

Just then, Patrolman Harvey got a call to respond to another accident a few miles away. "I'll take you back to headquarters, Mister Burke. The holding compound is on route 9 south, two miles from the headquarters building on the right hand side of the road at a Gulf service station."

"I understand. I'll take a look at it on my way back to Maine. I've got two children who have not heard about their mother. I need to go to them as soon as possible," Jon declared.

"If we can help you in any way possible, don't hesitate to call on us. You and your family have my sympathy. Here's a card of the service station that holds the crash vehicles," replied Patrolman Harvey.

Jon opened the door and shook the officer's hand. "You remind me of a first sergeant I had in Korea."

"I was in the Army, too. Tell the garage owner that I've authorized you to examine the vehicle. Good luck, Sir."

Jon slowly drove his truck down the road to the holding compound. He told the attendant who he was and what he wanted to do. The owner told him that Officer Harvey had called to make sure he had access to the vehicle. The kind policeman had again made things easy for him. He was most interested in viewing the passenger area where his wife was found. Broken glass was all over the interior. There was a depression on the dash where his Jill must have been pressed against it. It was painful to imagine the terror that must have been present split seconds before the impact of the truck.

Underneath the seat he found several scraps of paper with notes about repairs and maintenance of the Nash. Other scattered debris covered the floor. There was a large glove drawer in the center of the dashboard. It was bent partially open. He pried it open, and Jon found a small clutch bag he knew belonged to Jill because he had purchased it several years ago for her birthday. It brought tears to his eyes. He kissed it and placed it in his pocket. Why was it there in the glove box of a stranger?? Some of the cigarettes in the ash tray were the same as what Jill occasionally smoked after a meal. She was not addicted to them like most smokers.

The key was still in the ignition, and Jon took it to unlock the trunk of the Nash which was undamaged. There were two small overnight suitcases in the trunk. One belonged to Jill. He took it and walked to the truck with tears rolling down his chin. He told the attendant that he was taking the suitcase and the clutch. They belonged to his wife. The attendant told him it was okay. He sadly placed them on the floor of the passenger seat in the truck and started the engine.

The Buick, driven by the son called Alfred, came to a sudden stop beside Jon's truck. The son stared at the Nash, shook his head slowly, and buried it in his arms crossed on the steering wheel. Touched by his sadness, Jon started to get out of the truck and stopped. A little voice inside of him made him stop. What could he say to the young man? Platitudes were the last thing anyone wants to hear at such a painful time in their lives. He quickly got back in the truck and started the engine. He had a long, arduous trip ahead of him. The young man was about the same age as Carl who had yet to learn of his mother's sudden demise. Jon had his own family to take care of. He thought about his very precious and fragile Ashley and their three-month-old daughter, Nina, who had truly enriched their lives. Right now they were all the family he had left.

The ride to Durham, New Hampshire, was difficult. Carl Burke was enrolled in the four year forestry program. He was a good student in high school and a good basketball player even though he was not as tall as some of the players. He had inherited his mother's blond hair and blue eyes from her Finnish heritage. Jon and his son were very close. They went hunting and fishing together often. On days off from school, Carl worked frequently with his father in the field, surveying woodlots. Over the years, Jon and Carl had surveyed and documented thousands of acres of forestland in central and northern Maine. Forestry was a good fit for the serious young student.

Both Carl and Ashley had inherited their mother's spirited disposition. She was much more spontaneous than Jon, who had a tendency to be a loner, selecting his friends with care. At times when his reclusive nature was beginning to show itself, Jill would remind him of that fact and scold him. He never needed as much social interaction as Jill. It was not that he did not like people; he simply did not need them to function as much as she did.

The surveying business had supplied them with a reasonable standard of living. Jon was a demanding worker who put in twelve to sixteen hours of work every day in the field or in his office in the barn behind the house. After Jill had earned her engineering degree in design, she worked part-time setting herself up as a consultant. She did not like to fly and limited her work to the eastern half of the United States and Canada. Once her name became known, she was very much in demand. Her additional income added to the budget made life easier for the whole family.

Jon had insisted that the family buy a good, dependable automobile for Jill's traveling, and settled on a 1953 Studebaker President coupe with an automatic transmission. It had the same engine as Jon's truck. It was fast, comfortable and very well made. It was also a beautiful automobile. She loved it.

On the way to Durham, Jon mentally listed a number of things he had to do. Contacting Hastings Engineering was first on the list. He was wondering where the Studebaker coupe was parked and who was Lauren Hopkins? He was surprised that he was able to think so clearly. At some point after the funeral arrangements had been made for Jill, he wanted to talk to the truck driver in case something was missing in getting it second-hand from the police. He expected that the Hopkins family was having similar thoughts.

It was dark by the time Jon drove to the University of New Hampshire campus and parked off the main street beside Fairchild Hall where Carl lived. He was nervous and frightened at what he had to do. Carl's room was located on the basement floor of the building with two windows facing the road. Jon saw a light on in his room and went in to knock on the door.

"Who is it?" his son asked.

"It's me, Son," Jon replied.

Carl opened the door and embraced his father, happy to see him. Then, the look on his face and the lines under his eyes shocked him. "What's wrong, Dad? I called home a couple of times today, and nobody answered the phone. I called Ashley, and she had not heard from you. You look terrible, Dad. What's the matter?"

Jon held his son in a tight embrace and told him the truth. "I've come from New York upper state. Your mother was killed in a bad accident at Glens Falls early this morning. I rushed back to tell you. I haven't told Ashley yet."

The devastating news took a few moments to register with Carl. "Are you sure, Dad?" he cried.

"Yes, I've seen her body. There's no mistake, Son." He again grasped his son. They both wept until there were no tears left. "Gather what you need, Carl. We've got to tell Ashley and Hal. I'll need you with me."

"I can't believe it, Dad. Mom had promised that she would help me to use the slide rule this weekend." Carl told him, breaking down again.

Jon felt nakedly alone and helpless as he held his son's body, wracked with pain and disbelief, in his arms. "We've got to stick together if we're going to survive this ordeal, Son. How sad it is; your mother will never be able to watch little Nina grow up. At least she had her for a few months."

"I'd like to believe that Mom will be watching and caring, Dad."

"I really believe that, too, but it doesn't make the pain go away…"

"Have you eaten anything today, Dad?"

"No, I'm not hungry, Carl. Once we get to Ashley's I could use a cup of coffee. I just could not handle anything right now."

Jon told Carl that he had copies of all the reports available from the accident. He could review them later. They left the dormitory and placed the suitcase and bag of clothes behind the seat in the truck. The clutch was in the steel glove box on the dashboard. Neither Carl nor his father was prepared to examine the contents at this time. They would have to wait until they were better able to accept their loss.

Ashley and Hal Perkins lived at the shore near the old World War Two Coast Guard tower on a rocky point of land that jutted out from the shore. They had a nice view of the ocean. Hal was a State of Maine game warden for most of York County. He worked out of the State Police barracks on Route One towards Kennebunk. He was a highly decorated soldier from the Korean War. Jon and Jill were happy for the young couple. They liked Hal's easy-going ways. He was devoted to Nina and Ashley. Like most young couples with a new home mortgage, they had to be frugal to get by financially.

Ashley had inherited her mother's blond hair and blue eyes like Carl, but her personality was more in tune with her father. She had been a little shy growing up and, consequently, had formed a very close relationship to her mother. She was kind and caring and made a wonderful mother herself. Hal helped her to overcome some of her shyness. Little Nina was named after Jill's mother who had passed away several years before.

Jon was concerned that Hal might have known of the accident since he worked out of the same building as the State Police. Frequently he was alone somewhere within York County. The policeman that visited Jon may not have been from the Wells Barracks. He had not checked the card the policeman left with him early in the morning. Jon had an impression that he came from Augusta. He hoped that was the case, because he wanted to be the one to tell his daughter.

By the time Jon and his son reached Ashley's home at the beach, he was mentally and physically spent. Carl was worried about his father and insisted on driving the truck to Wells. His father let him and quietly sat reliving the chain of events that took his wife Jill away from him. They had a good marriage, and both seemed to be devoted to each other. They had been high school sweethearts, and Jill had supported him and kept the home fires burning all during the dark days of World War II and the Korean War. She was his life. He always had the feeling that he needed her more than she needed him. She was always more resourceful and self-sufficient than he was. How could he continue without her? How?

Chapter Three

Hal had seen the truck turn into the yard and met Carl and Jon at the door. "Say, this is a pleasant surprise," happily greeting them until he saw the look on both of their faces.

"We come with bad news, Hal. Is Ashley at home?" Jon embraced his son-in-law.

"She just finished Nina's bath. Come in. What is it, Jon?" Hal asked. He had never seen his father-in-law or his brother-in-law in such distress. He called out for Ashley. "Ashley, your father and brother are here."

Ashley ran in to the living room with Nina in her arms wrapped in a pink blanket. She was shocked by the terror she saw in her father's face.

"Ashley and Hal, you've got to be strong," Jon cried, releasing Hal and grasping Ashley and the baby. "I've just come from New York State. Your mother has been killed in an automobile accident..."

"No..." Ashley cried aloud, passing Nina to Hal. "No... she promised me that she'd take me shopping this weekend. No... it can't be..." she cried over and over again, scaring Nina who began to cry.

Jon held her close, and they wept in each other's arms.

Hal quieted Nina and placed her in the crib in the nursery so that she would not be upset anymore. He returned to the living room and tried to comfort Carl who was sitting on the couch holding his head in his hands. Convulsive shrieks and moans filled the room.

"Jill really liked that Studebaker President Coupe," commented Hal, controlling his emotions better than the others, taking a seat next to Carl on the couch. "My mother-in-law loved life so much, it's hard to reconcile that she's no longer with us."

"No, she did not have an accident in the coupe," corrected Jon. "She was a passenger in another person's car. I still don't know where her coupe is." Ashley heard the exchange between her father and her husband, but paid little attention to the details. All she knew was that her mother was dead – how or why she died wasn't important to her at this time.

"I'm going back to New York to search for some answers," announced Jon who had been quietly formulating a plan of action. "First I've got to arrange for her funeral and notify your cousins, aunts, and uncles on both sides of the family."

Hal saw an opportunity to be able to help his father-in-law. "Jon, I'm free of responsibilities for the weekend. Would it help if I went to New York with you? I could drive Jill's Studebaker back to Maine if you had other things you wanted to pursue. I'd like to help if I can."

"Your suggestion is a good one, Hal. I was contemplating sending it back via freight truck." Jon was pleased with the offer. "Could I bother you with a cup of coffee, maybe a sandwich or a sweet bite? I'm not really hungry, but I haven't eaten all day, and I know I've got to be strong to handle this crisis. Carl and I could bunk on your studio couch that folds out into a bed."

"Oh, yes, Father. I don't want to be alone tonight either. I just finished making a couple of apple pies from fresh Cortland apples that Hal and I picked a few days ago. We also have some strong cheddar cheese that has a little bit of a 'snap' that you like," replied Ashley, wiping her eyes and slowly walking to the kitchen, thankful for something to do to take her mind off the tragedy that had been thrust upon the family.

That night, Jon and his immediate family sat around the kitchen table and talked about events they remembered with Jill. It was a sobering time. Occasionally there was laughter interspersed with breakdowns of control. It was an unfamiliar world for the family, and they were unprepared for the depth of the pain that Jill's death created in each of them.

Throughout the evening Jon harbored worrisome questions that had plagued him ever since he learned of his wife's death. He kept the questions to himself so as to not violate the precious memories Ashley and Carl were in the process of renewing. Memories were all they had of their mother. Jon was never a jealous person, and his Jill never knowingly gave him cause to be suspicious or to question her word. The hurtful thoughts had to be confirmed or eliminated, or they would drive him crazy. The night was long and dark. Sleep on the pullout sofa came in short spurts interrupted by nostalgic memories they all shared.

Jon and Jill had been married for twenty-three years. Throughout the difficult war period, Jill had been supportive and faithful, writing almost every day to him while he was overseas. She kept the home fires burning for him like thousands of others experiencing the same thing, growing weary of the relentless fear of the unknown.

Jon woke to check his wristwatch. It was 3:30 AM, and he quietly rolled out of the bed and dressed. He went outside to his truck to check on the bag of clothes the pathologist had removed from Jill's body and the clutch bag he had retrieved from the wrecked Nash. The small purse held the registration for the Studebaker coupe and Jill's driver's license. Her wallet contained about a hundred dollars in assorted bills. Jon's hands were shaking in the cab of the truck with the dome light on. He kissed the leather bag he had given to her for a gift this past Christmas. When he emptied the contents on the seat several dollars worth of change fell out and a key with a name tag attached. He looked at the address on the key: Diamond Point Inn and Motel, 104 Shore Road, Diamond Point, New York – Suite #8.

He memorized the address and put everything back into the clutch. Then he grasped the bag of clothes, emptying them onto the seat, and was shocked by what he saw. Aside from the small evening jacket, the dress was a blue satin to match her blue eyes. He had never seen the dress before, never, he cried to himself. She never wore such an expensive dress with a revealing low cut to show much of her breasts. He was feeling painfully betrayed. There had to be some mistake. She never wore that dress in his presence, never! It was totally out of character for her to be seen in such a showy dress.

Hal was an early riser, and he noticed the light on in Jon's truck. He turned on the coffeemaker and went outside to see if Jon was all right. "I just put on a fresh pot of coffee." Jon was in his own world, and Hal saw the distress on his face. Looking at the colorful dress lying on the seat, Hal understood the cause and said, "Come inside, Jon."

"I couldn't wait any longer, Hal. I had to check these things. Now I wish I hadn't. From the very beginning there was something not right about the whole thing. I really don't care to get into it now, Hal. I've got to clarify several things with Hastings Engineering before I jump to any more conclusions. I believe Jill was involved with another man… My God, don't say anything to Ashley just now. The accident took place a hundred and fifty miles from the bridge she was called on to inspect. That fact has been bothering me from the start. If my instincts are correct, then I want you to promise me to keep it between the two of us."

"I can't believe I'm hearing this from you, Jon. Are you sure you're not letting your grief run wild with speculation? It's hard to imagine. Ashley would be sick if it was true. You can count on me, Jon. I agree with you. It's for the best to keep it that way." Hal helped him place the dress and jacket back into the paper bag.

"Let's have a coffee and a muffin, and then we can hit the road." Hal opened the door of the truck.

Jon followed him and embraced his son-in-law. "My daughter chose well. Thanks for the support. We'll leave Carl here with Ashley. A cup of coffee will go good, Hal."

"You've got to take care of yourself, Jon. I know it's difficult to eat when you're not hungry. Ashley made a batch of blueberry muffins yesterday. How about it?" Hal asked, pouring the coffee.

"To be honest, Hal, I prefer another piece of apple pie with a slice of cheese. Ashley turned out to be a good cook like her mother."

An hour later they were entering Vermont on their way west to Rutland. Shortly after that they passed into New York State through Fort Anne to U.S. Route 9 at Glens Falls. Jon motioned for Hal to pull off the road a short distance from Glens Falls where he pointed out the skid marks in the road and described how the accident unfolded. Hal acknowledged with a nod of his head and pulled back on the highway so as to not prolong the agony and to leave the scene to change Jon's mood.

Traffic slowed passing through Lake George. It was a busy village except in the dead of winter when the natives were able to reclaim their town. They left Route 9 and took the road to Fort Ticonderoga where they stopped for gasoline for the truck.

Hal asked the attendant for directions to the Diamond Point Inn and Motel on Shore Road. He told Hal it was just up the road on the right. It was an impressive Victorian style structure with several outlying buildings close to the water's edge.

Jon's first impression was that it was a very exclusive place with a large dining room which opened to a patio at the water's edge. He was holding the key to suite number eight. Hal parked the truck in the parking area and they walked around the corner of the motel units. Suddenly Jon's eyes lit up when he saw the Studebaker coupe parked beneath the pine trees. Hal looked at Jon. His face was chalk white.

"We better take this slow and easy, Jon. You don't look very good. I see number 8 ahead of us near the coupe," Hal remarked.

Jon removed the key from his pocket and opened the door to the suite. They were at the right place! Both of them cautiously stepped into the suite which had a large sitting room with a view of the water. The bedroom had been cleaned by the housekeeping people. A king-size bed dominated the room. It made Jon ill to look at it. Hal quickly checked all of the drawers in the bureaus and found them empty. The bathroom and kitchenette refuse cans were also empty. They found nothing that could point to the occupants.

Jon removed the keys in his pocket and handed them to Hal. "Check to see if the Studebaker has gas enough to make the trip back home."

Hal unlocked the door and started the V/8 engine in the coupe. He noticed that the gas tank was almost full, and oil pressure was normal, so he shut the engine down and walked back into the suite. Jon was sitting on a chair in the living room. There was a defeated look about him that worried Hal.

"The coupe is spotless, like Jill always kept it, and ready for the trip back to Maine," Hal announced.

"C'mon, Jon, let's get out of here. This place is poison for you."

Jon allowed himself to be led outside where he held out two sets of car keys. "Which vehicle do you want to drive back home, Jon?" Hal asked.

Numbed by the opulence of the inn and motel, Jon took the truck keys. "I'll use the truck, Hal. You can take the coupe back with you. I've got some things I want to check out. I need to bring this nightmare to a logical conclusion and may be a couple more days, depending on what I find. I promise to call your place every day. Thanks for the help, Hal. I'll be all right. Right now I'm more angry than I am sorrowful. Do you have enough money to make it back home?"

"Sure I do, but I don't want to leave you here alone. I understand your desire to learn everything possible pertaining to the accident, but beating the same old dog can be hurtful and accomplish nothing except more heartache. I can't tell you that it's right or wrong. I'm just concerned for you, Jon. I'll do whatever you wish."

Jon hugged Hal. "This is the most vicious time I've ever experienced. Combat was easy compared to this. I've simply got to know more of why and what happened here with Jill. I plan to contact Hastings Engineering, and I must learn more about this Lauren Hopkins. When I've exhausted any information available, I'll come home, Hal. Have a safe trip."

"You know we'll be worrying about you until that time comes."

"I know that. First, I'm going to return the key to the suite. Wish me luck, Hal."

Jon watched Hal drive the coupe down to the main road and turn left out of sight. He had never seen the coupe without Jill driving it, and it pained him even more, feeling empty and alone. He was proud of how steadfast his son-in-law was in a crisis situation. He understood how he was such a successful and well-liked game warden. Jon entered the main lobby to return the key to the suite, hoping to solicit more information about the recent occupants in the suite.

Jon stepped to the desk to tell the clerk about the accident. The clerk had not heard about it and told Jon that the bill had just been paid by a Mrs. Hopkins. Jon turned to see Mrs. Hopkins standing by the door looking at him.

Chapter Four

Mrs. Amber Hopkins had that same depressed and bewildered look of desperation he had seen when she showed up at the accident site yesterday. She turned to speak to him with trembling lips, and nothing came out. Tears streamed down her face as she walked out the door of the lobby.

Jon knew what she was going through and followed her out the door. "Please don't leave, Mrs. Hopkins. I need to talk to you... someone, or I'll go mad. I, too, share the horror I see in your eyes. I can't make any sense or reason out of what we've had to deal with."

He led her to a bench close to the water's edge beneath a clump of white pine trees. She nodded her head in agreement. They needed to talk. They both sat quietly for a few minutes staring across the water at the Green Mountains in Vermont. The peaceful scene was in direct contrast to the fury that was raging in their souls.

"As you have probably already determined," Jon began, measuring his words carefully, "I'm Jon Burke. Jill was my wife for twenty-three years and the mother of our two children. You and I are victims of a cruel and deceptive attack on our sanity. I almost feel as if I had to apologize for my wife's transgressions... My God, where did I fail her? What did I do or fail to do that could have triggered such a sham? I wouldn't be surprised that you are experiencing the same feeling of helplessness, anger and despair."

Amber Hopkins blew her nose and wiped the tears from her face with a lace handkerchief. "It's strange, but, yes, I've had similar thoughts. Lauren was far from being a perfect man, but a relation of this proportion is beyond my ability to understand."

"Tell me, Mrs. Hopkins, did your husband ever work for Hastings Engineering?" Jon asked.

22

"Yes, two years ago he was relieved from that company. He soon took another job at a mechanical engineering firm. I contacted Hastings to find out all that I could about your wife, Jill. They had worked together often on the same projects. Just how long their relationship had been going on had been a mystery to me until I learned that the suite here in Lake George has been leased for the past two years. So, we can conclude that their affair is at least two years old… Not very encouraging, is it? What a fool I was. I gave him everything he asked for and not once questioned him. I was stupid, blind, and way too generous with money. It appears that I have been supporting their clandestine meetings…" She began to weep again and buried her face in her hands.

Mrs. Hopkins had answered most of his questions. The lady sitting on the bench beside him was traumatized by the magnitude of their mates' unfaithfulness. Perhaps Jill and Lauren had sat on the same bench looking at the same view across the water! Two innocent families had to the pay the price. It was grossly unfair and undeserved.

He placed a comforting hand on Mrs. Hopkins' shoulder and cried partly to himself, "I don't know if I should cry or scream; I've never felt so violated. I'm angry, hurt, and outraged all at the same time, and I keep asking the same question over and over again…Why?"

Amber Hopkins listened to his words and exclaimed, "That question erodes my faith in a just God. I keep searching for answers but come up empty."

"We're paying the penalty for their actions," Jon replied. "The night before she left we had been planning a trip up to Moosehead Lake in northern Maine. Not once did I detect duplicity or insincerity… not ever! Was I blind or just plain stupid?"

"We were neither, Jon Burke. We were simply trusting in those whom we believed to be trustworthy. They were living a lie. Our trust enabled them to betray us because we were unprepared to assign such actions to the ones we loved. Lauren had always gambled too much, but I never complained. It was only money, and he was good to Alfred and the twin girls we had two years after Alfred was born. The children are the ones who will feel the most betrayed. 'Stupid Amber' couldn't figure it out, and I paid all of his bills for him. I now acknowledge that he married me only for the money I inherited. He liked the good life, which is okay, but it doesn't buy happiness. I was a colossal fool…"

"No, Mrs. Hopkins, you were simply trusting your mate. I never dreamed that Jill could be a party to such open treachery! This conversation has answered a lot of my questions. I thank you for that. Explaining it to the children will be the hardest part. My son-in-law drove Jill's car back to Maine for me. Now I can follow him. There's nothing left to learn about this affair."

"My son, Alfred, has taken this very hard. He needs me now more than ever. I should get back to Albany," Mrs. Hopkins said in a calmer voice. "Our conversation has helped a lot. I blamed your wife for Lauren's unfaithfulness, and that was unfair. Now, both of them have paid the heavy price for their acts, but the burden of grief will be borne by the innocent. It's just not fair."

"Thanks for sharing your thoughts and information with me, Mrs. Hopkins. I've already concluded that I'm not going to tell the whole truth to the children. Nothing positive will be gained if I shared the truth. That also goes for friends and family members. By being silent, I can save a lot of people the heartache you and I are having trouble accepting. The truth would only hurt. My Jill was not the same woman that was sneaking around meeting your husband. The sexy, expensive, and showy clothes she was wearing when they had the accident were completely different from her normal wardrobe," Jon exclaimed breathlessly.

"I'm not surprised. That was what he liked. Evidently I was not enough for him. What I wouldn't give to be able to confront him with his sneaky escapades! How I hate him and your wife for doing this to two innocent families. Maybe God did punish them, but that doesn't make it easier to accept or to live with. I should be getting back to Albany. There's much to be done. I'm also thankful that we had a chance to talk, Mr. Burke."

Jon searched for the truck keys in his pocket. "By the way, when was the last time you had anything to eat, Mrs. Hopkins?"

"Food has been the last thing on my mind," she replied calmly.

"I understand, but more than ever, we have to take care of ourselves and be strong. May I buy each of us a light lunch?

24

Lake George is full of good restaurants." Jon stood up from the bench.

"My son scolded me this morning for not eating," she replied to his offer. "Yes, I think we should take some nourishment. You pick the place, and I'll follow your red truck. It's a distinctive vehicle."

"I'm a Studebaker enthusiast," he smiled. "I noticed a nice Italian restaurant on the left just after the pavilion where the fort is being built. I like pizza. How does that sound?"

"That's as good as any," she replied, starting towards her Buick.

They parked at the restaurant side by side. Jon walked over to open the Buick's door for her. It was a natural instinct for him. He had always done it for his mother, Jill, his mother-in-law and any other woman he knew. "When we're done I may go over to check out the construction of the old fort. I'm an avid history buff and have studied the French and Indian War and the Revolutionary War as they took place in the Champlain-Hudson Valley area. The movie, *Last of the Mohicans,* was all about the French capture of Fort William Henry at Lake George."

They entered the restaurant together and were seated at a window looking out towards the fort under construction. She quickly excused herself and went to the restroom. The waiter came, and Jon told him they'd order as soon as the lady returned. She had combed her hair and pulled it behind her ears, falling loose about her shoulders. She was still a little uncomfortable in his presence. When the waiter took their order she asked for minestrone soup, a salad and coffee.

"What do you say if we have a truce and don't talk about the death of our spouses and the circumstances that surrounded it?" he asked, sitting across the table from her.

"That sounds like a good idea to me. I'm exhausted," she replied, adding sugar to her coffee the waiter had just poured for both of them. "By the way, what do you do for work?"

"I'm a self-employed land surveyor. I started the business right after I got out of the Army in 1945. Five years later, I was recalled to duty in Korea. I was tempted to make a career out of the Army. I had been given a battlefield commission and was in command of a company with the rank of captain. After talking it over with Jill, I decided to continue with my survey work, so as to be at home more with the kids growing up and all. I still keep abreast of military affairs in the Maine National Guard."

"Your address is Wells, Maine. Are you on the coast?" she asked.

"No, our daughter Ashley and her husband have purchased a year-round home on the coast. I live five miles inland in a rural area. We have several hundred acres of forestland. I'm managing the land so that it will financially help me when I retire or cannot physically work like I do now. I can't believe that I'm telling you these things." He shook his head.

"Do you miss not being in the Army?" she asked in a clear voice.

"I was blessed with the command of some magnificent men who have eternally earned my respect and admiration. I was also lucky to have survived two wars unscathed. Yes, at times I miss the camaraderie that exists in the Army; that's the main reason I maintained skills in the National Guard. Now, that's enough about me, what about you, Mrs. Hopkins? I suspect that we come from two distinct and different social circles," he commented.

She sipped her coffee and picked at her salad as if it tasted good to her. "This is the first thing I've eaten since I heard of the accident. My father was a career Army officer who retired as a major general several years ago. His father was a very successful manufacturer of medical instruments and supplies, so I guess you could say that I had the benefit of wealth, but it did not take me long to learn that it also demanded responsibility and an appreciation that money has to be earned; it's not a gift. My father was a humble man who lived his life by the code he embraced at the Military Academy at West Point – duty, honor, country. We probably lived as frugally as you did, Mister Burke."

"I've known officers like that. How fortunate you were."

"As for me, I studied at the University of Virginia in Charlottesville for a degree in education. When I graduated, I was the only person in the family available to care for my mother who was very ill with leukemia. I looked after her for several years until the disease took her. My father retired from the Army shortly after that. I had already met Lauren at school and dated him often. We were married a year later. I can honestly say that it was not an unhappy arrangement.

"However, I became aware of his unfaithfulness long before your wife Jill entered the picture. When he was with us, he was a good father, and I was able to forgive his transgressions for the sake of the children. Things really changed for the worse when he was relieved of his engineering job by Hastings. I was never told of the reason, but he soon took a job at a firm in Albany. I suspect that your wife and he saw each other much more often than we imagined. My son and twin girls had no idea what was taking place. The children never knew, and I do not plan to tell them."

"I saw your son, Alfred, at the compound where the Nash was stored. He was suffering, and my heart went out to him."

"They are the reason this seems so unfair. The innocent suffer the most. I wish I could be a good Christian and forgive Lauren and your wife, but I just can't, not now. I hate her for the pain she has inflicted on my family. Sure, Lauren shares the blame, too. It takes two willing people to carry out the deception they planned and executed."

She spoke with conviction. Her eyes reflected the hurt and anger that was consuming her. Jon had similar feelings, but she was able to verbalize them better. "I understand, Mrs. Hopkins, and I agree with you. I'm glad we had a chance to meet and to talk without assigning blame. We both have a very painful duty ahead of us, and I want you to know that I will pray that God will guide you over this difficult road we must travel. Words don't help much, and well-meaning platitudes are worthless."

"The funeral will be a stressful ordeal," she replied, avoiding his study of her. "I must be getting back to Albany. I've received answers to most of my questions except the biggest one of all… how did I fail Lauren so that he found the need to seek love and companionship with another woman? The question will haunt me for a long time."

Jon thought she had succinctly compressed the pain and hurt in a simple question that neither of them could answer. He had been entertaining the same powerful questions in search of answers.

"What else can be said, Mrs. Hopkins?" he asked helplessly. "This is the first time I've been able to think rationally about what has taken place since the notification by the Maine State Police. Thank you for sharing some thoughts with me. May I have the privilege of paying for lunch since I asked you?"

"If you insist," she replied, blowing her nose with a tissue from her purse. "Thank you for suggesting it. Drive carefully; it's a long ways to drive under these circumstances. I'll be home within an hour. Good-bye, Jon Burke. Your wife was a fool. She picked a loser in Lauren, and so did I."

"Good-bye, Mrs. Hopkins." He opened the door for her from the restaurant and held the Buick door for her to get into the vehicle. The two deeply disturbed individuals then went their separate ways...

Chapter Five

It was midnight before Jon arrived at his daughter's home. The outside light had been left on to greet him. He smiled. It was typical of Hal and Ashley. Not wanting to wake anyone, he quietly let himself in and undressed in the living room where Carl was sleeping on the pullout sofa. He was mentally and physically exhausted. Carl was sprawled over most of the bed. Knowing that his son was a heavy sleeper, he gently turned him over to make room. The clean smell of the ocean filled the room from two open windows. Jon tried to plan the next few days ahead of him, but he soon fell asleep in spite of the ugly images that filtered through his consciousness. Exhaustion had claimed him completely.

That next morning, Jon was up early and had coffee with Hal, asking him if he had said anything to Ashley or Carl.

Hal whispered in his ear, "I never said a word about Lake George or the relationship between Jill and Lauren. I promise to keep the painful truth from the family. Nothing is accomplished by sharing the bad news."

Jon agreed. "This Lauren can be explained by the fact that he was employed by Hastings the same as Jill. That's the truth."

The two shook hands. Both of them were relieved that they would not have to share the real story with their loved ones. It would eliminate a lot of unnecessary explanations that were too painful to even think about and could only injure the rest of the family.

Jon's first order of business was to call the local Methodist minister and the funeral home for funeral arrangements. He and Jill had always planned on being buried at the large cemetery across Route One from the high school. He dropped off the clothes Ashley had selected for her mother at the undertaker's office. Her wedding ring was included in the package the coroner had given him at Glens Falls. The most difficult task he had to perform was to select a casket for his wife. The room displaying several styles and ranges in price wreaked of death. Jon was not sure he was going to make it through the selection ordeal. The local undertaker, an old classmate, helped him make the decision that would please Jill. It made him ask just which Jill was he going to bury? He was still white as a sheet when Ashley met him at the door.

The two-day wait for the undertaker to get Jill's body and prepare for the services was an eternity to Jon and the family. Carl and Ashley held up better than their father. Cousins, aunts and uncles from both families stayed with Ashley and at Jon's home in the Highpine region of Wells. Many of Jill's family members had driven from Bangor to attend the services. Jon had selected six men to be the pallbearers, two from each family and two Army officers from the National Guard that knew Jon.

The night before the funeral, Jon spent a difficult night remembering how it had been for him and Jill. They had been together over two decades, and he could never recall a time when he felt that Jill had ever been unfaithful to him. Even during the tumultuous war years, she had been steadfast and loyal to their commitment to each other. In the darkest hours of the brutal campaigns through Africa, Sicily, Italy, and ultimately Europe, her letters never failed to comfort and sustain him when he was frightened, cold, and hungry.

She wrote every day filling him in on the local news and gossip and how the children were progressing in school. It was almost as if Jill had been two different people. The Jill he married and who bravely faced the challenges of maintaining the home front during his long absences was not the same person that the accident in New York had revealed to him. What had he done wrong that had tempted his Jill to stray and violate everything they held sacred? That searching question was driving him crazy!

He had a hard time with family members. They all were entitled to the truth, but he was so certain it would only add to their sadness that he rationalized successfully for denial of the sordid facts. His deception made him wonder if he had told them the truth if they would even believe it. He himself was having trouble reconciling that fact of life, so he suffered in silence and asked God to give him the strength to get through the funeral and the committal services. He desperately needed to be alone. Small talk to fill up the day was driving him crazy. He wanted everyone to leave so that he could be alone to calm the turmoil within his heart. How could he plot a future without Jill at his side? He hated her and loved her at the same time.

Ashley and Carl recognized that their father was on the verge of a breakdown. The look on his face frightened both of them. They tried to shelter him as much as possible from the large number of people who wished to express their sympathies to him. Hal, always faithful, had been at his side for much of the day.

The funeral director had informed Jon that he would provide as much time as the family needed for a private viewing of the deceased before he admitted the general public. They all accepted the opportunity with gratitude to spend a few quiet moments with their beloved. Jill was dressed in appropriate and familiar clothes Ashley had selected, including a light green blouse and a dark green blazer to complement Jill's blond hair with strands of gray. The familiar clothes made her seem real and alive. Jon's first impression was that the undertaker had done a good job of hiding the bad bruise on her forehead where she had hit the windshield. For a split moment he thought it might all be a bad dream, and she was going to open her eyes and speak to them. Similar thoughts passed through the entire family, but the cold pallor on her face quickly dispelled any remaining hopes and prayers. Jill had a light amount of lipstick which was normal for her.

Ashley was the first to completely break down. Gasping sobs filled the quiet room. Hal rushed to support his wife. Wrapping his arms around her, he led her to a nearby chair. Carl and Jon followed her to the stability of the chairs. All eyes were locked on the inert figure in the casket before them. They stayed in the room venting their grief and finally had to accept the fact that she was no longer going to be with them. Death was permanent. As hard as it was for Ashley and Carl, they both knew that it was more of an ordeal for their gentle father. He had held himself in control in front of others, but the horror they saw in his eyes and the firm muscles about his mouth told them that he needed release. They had never seen him like this, and he could not tell them what was hurting the most!

The funeral director entered the room to see if anybody needed anything. They all stood quietly at the casket and said good-bye before leaving the room. Jon noted that she was wearing the wedding ring Ashley had included in the clothing bundle for the director. He leaned over the casket to kiss the ring and to kiss Jill's cold brow and whispered: "Good-bye, My... love... good-bye... Why Jill? Why...?" The words choked him...

The minister of the Church Jill and Jon had attended held the services. The minister stressed that the Jill he knew would want the people who were now mourning her demise to continue their lives and not be saddened by her death. He stressed that she was now at peace.

That night after the funeral, Jon wished the large numbers of mourners a safe drive back home and waved farewell. He was relieved to be alone. Many times during the past two days, he questioned his ability to make it without a complete meltdown. Food of every description was supplied by loved ones and neighbors. Jon gently told them to desist. He was not in the mood to eat.

Carl and Ashley had sorted out the mail with cards in one pile on Jon's desk in the little office he had built into the shed off the kitchen. Late that night, Jon thumbed through the cards and was surprised to find one from Glenn Hastings, owner of Hastings Engineering. He opened it and read a sincere note how they had valued her competent professionalism. Their loss of a mother and a soul mate was shared by many people in the company who knew Jill. Jon had met Glenn Hastings and knew that his message was sincere.

Near the bottom of the pile, Jon saw a card from Amber Hopkins. He had sent one to her out of respect for the family's loss. He would tell the children who she was if they asked, but so far, he and Hal had been successful in shielding the rest of the family from the full truth. The children were in enough pain. They didn't need information that would taint every warm memory they had of their mother. He was proud of the way Hal had stood by him in making that decision. His marriage to Ashley was a blessing for everyone. Ashley worshipped him for his kind and caring ways. Carl loved him like a brother.

Late into the evening, Jon pushed the cards to one side and sat with his feet on the old desk asking himself the age old question: "Where do we go from here?"

Jon knew himself well enough that if he kept busy at things that needed to be done, it would help him to accept the greatest loss in his life. Jill had been a wife, lover, mother, and the one person who gave meaning to his existence. Ashley and Carl needed him more than ever, and he was resolved to be available to them more than he had in the past. He would remain silent about their mother who had destroyed years of soft memories they had shared. She had also destroyed a lifetime of sharing as completely as she had destroyed herself and any ounce of respect he held for her. It was a cruel position for him to accept, and he knew it would be even worse for the children to handle if they knew the truth.

How he loathed her for betraying his trust and faith in her. For him to dedicate his life to her memory would be impossible. The act of love would only give approval of her conduct and callous disregard to their marriage vows. The duplicity bothered him the most because he could not confront her for an answer…why? He knew that he had to root the hatred out of his soul, for it was a poison that would kill him, too. He had to find a way to put his life back together, and he was the only one capable of climbing that mountain.

The day after the funeral service, Jon and Carl woke to a bright, sunny day. Warm days in September were always welcome to those who were not anxious for the long months of winter in Maine. Father and son decided to go out into the woodlot to cut firewood for the wood stove in the kitchen and the fireplace in the living room. Over the years, Jon had maintained a steady supply of well-seasoned firewood for the house as well as four cords for Ashley and Hal to burn in their fireplace at the beach. The production of firewood on the property was a constant work-in-progress.

The forestland was a mixture of white pine, hemlock and assorted hardwoods. Jon applied his stewardship to those areas where harvesting could benefit the residual stand. That way he was able to produce hardwood firewood and improve the growing stock of the forest at the same time. A win/win situation! There was a ready market for white pine logs anytime he wished to harvest a load or two to help pay annual property taxes. The forest as a whole was growing more than they were able to harvest, so the value of the improved growing stock was increasing by about six percent each year.

There was a stand of large white pine trees on the eastern boundary line of about ten acres that was always an inspiration to him. They were all over three feet in diameter at breast height and towered over much of the forest. He had estimated that most of the trees within the stand were capable of producing six sixteen foot-logs per tree. He never had the heart to cut them. They stood like sentinels guarding the fortress, and he had solved most of his bothersome problems within the confines of their majesty. He always felt a sense of awe when he walked beneath their towering canopies, and a soothing sense of peace came over him. Today he needed their healing power more than ever, and he sought their shelter with a desperate heart filled with pain.

Jon firmly believed that the tranquility of the forest helped him to maintain his sanity over the years. Like all veterans he was still troubled by images of combat in the two wars he had experienced. He never shared the effect they had on him with anyone, even Jill. First it was too painful to describe, and he could never put the images into words. It was too complicated. Occasionally when two veterans got together, they could talk about what had taken place in combat. Only another veteran could ever know. The brotherhood of combat veterans was a large fraternity who suffered in silence. There were few outlets for release of the pain in civilian life.

When Jon returned from the wars he had sought the sanctuary of peace in the forest, specifically the stand of large white pine trees that had stood the test of time amidst decades of fierce winters with deep snow and heavy winds. Yet, they remained stalwart and still towered above the rest of the land. He had a desperate need for release of the turmoil. He was never disappointed and came away richer and stronger than when he entered the citadel beneath the spreading canopies.

For days Jon was anxious to seek the sanctuary where he often just sat and remembered how it was and why they had fought so courageously for the right to be free from tyranny. It was a noble cause, and the price of victory was high, measured by the tears of bereaved mothers and loved ones. He had survived the crucible, and that was reward enough. The memories could never be erased or shared, and they were minimized by the same courage and determination that had been displayed on the battlefield. Once he was alone in the forest, Jon was able to communicate with his God easier than he could in a church. It defied logic, but it was the truth.

The physical effort required to cut firewood helped to relieve his anxieties. He always returned to the house a better man more in control of his emotions. Ashley and Hal were pleased when they saw him and Carl leave the house for the well-worn path out to the majestic pine stand. That spring Jon had purchased a new Homelite direct drive chain saw with an eighteen inch cutting bar. It was capable of cutting through an oak stem much quicker than the older gear drive saw he had started with after the war. He and Carl had often worked together felling trees and cutting them to proper length for the stove and fireplace.

They entered a stand of mixed hardwood and pine with a sprinkling of hemlock. If they removed the overtopping hardwoods, the younger pine seedlings would grow faster once they were released. Jon liked to cut firewood and left the area as productive as ever. Any single acre of land will grow a certain amount of wood fiber. If that growth could be concentrated on those species of trees which were the most merchantable, the productivity of the site was improved. Thinning a stand of trees accomplishes the same thing as a row of carrots in a garden. If the owner does not remove a portion of the carrots stems, the land will produce a lot of small carrots. If they are properly thinned at a young age, they will produce fewer, but larger carrots. That concept works for all of nature. The struggle for air and water is a constant dynamic.

Jon and Carl cut several oak and maple trees that were competing with the residual young white pine trees. Once the trees were on the ground, they would cut them into eighteen inches lengths for the parlor stove, and twenty-four inches for the fireplace. The wood was thrown into piles close to the forest track they would clear so that they could drive the faithful old Farmall. A tractor with a ten foot trailer along the roadway to pick up the wood.

They carried a small backpack with lunch, consisting of two sandwiches each and a thermos of coffee. Carl also included several home-made donuts one of the neighbors had left in the kitchen for them. They worked diligently until late in the morning when they took a welcome break for lunch. Work in the woods always produced a healthy appetite. The food tasted good. It was the first time Carl saw his father act as if he was hungry since the accident. The forest was working its magic on him.

The first tree they selected to cut down after lunch was a red maple about ten inches in diameter. Jon had sized it up so that he could drop it in a clear spot beside two hemlock trees. Directing Carl a safe distance away, Jon started the new direct drive chain saw and made a notch to direct the tree where he wanted it to fall. The saw was faster than he judged, and he had completely cut the stem from the stump. Normally he would have left a narrow band of wood to act as a hinge to direct the tree to the chosen spot. The top of the maple hit one of the hemlock trees, forcing the butt end of the tree off the stump opposite the direction of the top. It hit Jon's foot, pushing it against another tree close by before the tree rolled off the hemlock to the ground. Jon was not quick enough to get his foot out of the way. It was wedged against the pine tree and partially forced into the soft ground. It took all of Jon's strength to pull it from the vice that held it fast.

Carl saw what was happening and had yelled for his dad to move, but the warning was not quick enough. He ran to help his father, shutting down the saw first. Once his foot was free, Jon sat on the ground, unable to stand. It was a long way back to the house, and Carl told his father that he was going to get the wheelbarrow to help carry him out of the woods.

An hour later, they were sitting in the kitchen where Carl gently removed his father's socks and steel-toe boot. The ankle and foot had swollen to twice their normal size and were completely black and blue. Sharp pains ran through Jon's leg, and he laid on the floor and passed out. His face was as white as a sheet and his eyes rolled, showing the white to the frightened Carl.

Chapter Six

"You've got to have your foot x-rayed, Dad," Carl demanded when his father opened his eyes a few moments later. "You may have some broken bones. Looks as if you're going to be laid up for a while."

"Who would think that such a small tree could pack such a punch?" Jon said, trying to make light of it. "I agree, Carl. We should see a doctor. The York hospital is the closest for us. Do you want to chauffeur your father in the coupe?"

"Sure, the sooner the better, Dad. I'll wash up a little and get the coupe out of the garage. Mom really liked that car. I think those Studebaker coupes are the prettiest cars on the road."

"I don't disagree with you, Son," Jon replied, trying to place a sock on his injured foot. "I need this like a hole in the head," he sighed.

Carl had been driving since he was fifteen. He took his driver's license test in the family's 1948 Studebaker Champion which had the famous hill-hold brake system. They worked great for starting and stopping on a hill. Once you stopped the automobile you could take your foot off the brake pedal, and the car did not roll backwards until you released the clutch. One test that every driver had to pass on a steep hill was to not roll backwards from a stop more than six inches. The state inspector did not realize that the Studebaker was equipped with the famous hill-holding system. He remarked to Carl that it was the best stop and start technique he had experienced. Carl had smiled and said nothing about the unique Studebaker engineering feature.

The York Village hospital was the closest facility from Wells. Carl skillfully parked the coupe at the front entrance to the hospital and rushed in to get a wheelchair for his father. Two aides came out to wheel him into an examination room.

The doctor on duty took one look at the swollen ankle and ordered X-rays.

"You seem to be in pain, Mr. Burke. Your foot must have taken a hard blow to end up looking like that. Sometimes a bruised or sprained foot is longer to heal and more painful than a broken bone. We'll soon know if you did break anything. I'll give you something for the pain as soon as we examine the pictures of your foot."

"Whatever you say, doctor." Jon replied, feeling helpless. What an inconvenience this was going to be at this trying time for the family! Carl was in the waiting room where he called Ashley to explain what had happened.

While Carl was talking with Ashley, his father was removed from the X-ray room to a private one where the doctor administered a sedative to settle Jon's nerves and to ease the pain. He did have one broken toe, but it would mend in time. The rest of the foot and ankle were badly bruised. A nurse began to wrap it in ice packs to halt the swelling. She had told Carl that he could be with his father now.

"Your father will be resting for a couple of hours," the doctor told Carl. "You can take him home after he gains consciousness. I'll give you a prescription for codeine medication to take at night so that he can sleep."

While the doctor was talking to Carl, Hal entered the room to check on Jon's condition. The doctor told him what the X-rays showed and that he could go home. His ankle would take several weeks to heal and suggested alternating warm Epsom salts baths with cool water baths with a few ice cubes. Both would accelerate healing and ease the pain.

"Thanks, doctor," Hal said, placing an arm around Carl's shoulder. "You've had a busy day, Carl. Ashley called me on my radio. I was nearby and decided to check on Jon. You did the right thing getting him here. You look as if you could use a coffee. Let's grab one here at the coffee shop. How do you like the way that Studebaker coupe goes over the road? What a handsome automobile."

Carl smiled. "It would be an easy car to get a ticket with. Ma had a heavy foot sometimes. I'm surprised that she never got stopped."

While Carl and Hal were having coffee and donuts, a nurse entered Jon's room, looking at the chart at the foot of the bed. "Good Lord, it's Jon Burke," she exclaimed.

Jon heard his name as if he was in a fog and far away, but he recognized the voice. It was Joan Adams, a classmate from Wells High School. He had not seen her in years. She bent over him and took his pulse. She then listened to his heartbeat and gently placed a thermometer in his mouth.

"Is that you, Joan?" he asked with a thick tongue.

"I'm sorry if I disturbed your rest, Jon. Yes, this is Joan. The doctor said you had an unfortunate accident. We want to thoroughly check you so that your son in the coffee shop can take you home. I read about Jill in the paper, and I'm so sorry for you and your family. I liked her and was proud to call her a friend. We got together often when both of us were at college."

"Hi, Joan. It's nice to see a friendly face. I had a disagreement with an oak tree, and the tree won. This will take me out of commission for a while."

"I recognized your name on the chart, Jon. You'll need a good rest; that's for sure. I've got to get back to my floor. I noticed your son, Carl, in the coffee shop. I wish you and your family all the best, dear friend. You've got a lot of friends who are praying for you, and that includes me."

"Thanks, Joan. I'll take all the prayers I can get. It's nice to know you're not alone. Compared to my experience in two wars, I can tell you that this will be the hardest mountain to climb…thanks, Joan…"

She kissed him on the forehead and left the room. She had known Jon ever since they attended the first grade, and had never seen him so drained and forlorn. She knew how close the family was, and that pleased her. She did not know Hal, who was with Carl, except by reputation. The sturdy warden was known for his sense of fair play and commitment to the laws he enforced. He brought dignity and respect to the uniform.

Jon had fallen asleep when Joan left him and slept until eight o'clock that evening. Hal had to leave and promised to check in on them in the morning. He joked with Carl before leaving. "If you have to make coffee for your father, measure out the coffee and water carefully. He's very particular about his coffee. Sometimes your mother made it too weak, and your father called it 'troubled water'. If you're not sure, err on the side of stronger instead of weaker."

"Thanks, Hal. I'll remember that. I'll see that he gets home okay. I have a feeling this is going to be a long, difficult period for him," Carl predicted.

"You might consider staying with Ashley and me anytime. I've got to run. See you, Carl."

"Be careful out there, Hal."

Carl and his father left the hospital a couple of hours later, driving through York Harbor and Long Sands Beach to the Nubble Lighthouse. It was dark, and the light shone brightly on the parking area. Carl parked the Studebaker and rolled down the window to smell the fresh scent of the Atlantic.

"I used to come here often after the Second World War," Jon reminded Carl. "It was a place where I could sit in peace and contemplate where I'd been and where I was going. I found the same kind of peace here as I do at our stand of virgin white pine at home."

"I've never heard you talk about the war, Dad. I've discussed it with classmates at school, and those who have had loved ones in the war say the same thing about them," Carl said, hoping that this might be the moment when his father would open up on the subject.

Jon turned to look across the dark Atlantic as if he was searching for something. "There are some things that are difficult to put into words, and probably it's for the best if it remains that way. I lost a lot of good men in Korea, but the prolonged combat over years in the Second War was the most difficult. I was a platoon sergeant for most of the war. Platoons and companies are the tip of the spear against enemy strongholds. It was kill or be killed. Death and destruction were commonplace. Only another soldier who has experienced it can truly relate to what it was like. Those who have been to the edge of the volcano know and understand the reticence to discuss it with loved ones. I can't tell you any more than that, Carl. I pray that you'll never have to experience such things."

"I enjoy the ROTC (Reserve Officer Training Corps) at school. There's one sergeant with a chest full of ribbons and hash marks that cover the sleeve of his left arm. He seems to know what he's talking about and is very popular with the students."

"I'm sure he is, Son. I had it a lot easier in Korea after I received my commission as a second lieutenant in charge of a platoon of about fifty men, but I missed the camaraderie that existed at the enlisted man's level. You'll learn about unit cohesion in the Army. Without that ability to work as a team, platoons and companies would be nothing more than mobs instead of the disciplined organizations they are. The unique brotherhood or fraternity of veterans who share the same fears; the same commitment to accomplish the mission; and the same horror that is commonplace on the battlefield all bind them together as nothing in the civilian world is capable of doing."

"Were you ever scared, Dad?"

"Every day in combat, Carl. Fear is not a bad thing. It helps to heighten your awareness of things around you. Those instincts save lives," Jon replied not wanting to continue the conversation. "Let's go home, Son. I'm getting tired."

Jon did not say anything to his son, but the Nubble Lighthouse was a popular destination for Jill and him. It brought back a lot of warm memories that invited tears. He recalled one time when they were parked in the same place before the war started in their 1937 Lafayette sedan. They had watched two Coast Guardsmen pull themselves across the deep divide in a box suspended from a wire cable and make their way to the light house lantern and ignite it. Once it was lit, they returned across to the parking area.

It was that time when Jill had mentioned the story of a couple she knew who had just filed for a divorce. Both parties were unfaithful to each other. Jill had asked him in a teasing manner: "What would you do if I was attracted to another man?"

He had brushed it off lightly by telling her the truth. "I'd be long gone, leaving you with your lover. Maybe some couples could survive such indiscretions; as for me, I'd walk away without looking back."

Jill had laughed and cuddled him, as she often did, and laid her head against his chest. "I'm a lucky woman."

Jon could still hear her voice the way it was back then. Now he pondered the incident. Was there a part of his Jill that he had never discovered? He was thankful that Carl could not see the tears that clouded his vision. Life without his Jill would be lonely. The fact that she had been living a lie shattered what he had believed was uniquely his own all through the years. That corrupted every precious memory of Jill that he had treasured over the years of separation in two wars. He had felt himself to be lucky. Her betrayal robbed him of self-respect and filled him with questions without answers. Was it that easy for her to find solace in another man's arms? That question was driving him close to the edge!

Chapter Seven

Two Years Later, July 1957

Carl was working with his father for the summer to earn some money. He had recently taken a course in Civil Engineering for his degree in forestry. Therefore, he was able to use the transits his father used on a daily basis. Jon had received a contract from the St. Regis Paper Company in Millinocket, Maine, for the perimeter survey and subdivision of several thousand acres of land they had purchased from the Great Northern Paper Company which was going out of business. The subdivisions were made up of the various watershed areas within the region. The plot of land included several bodies of water including streams, ponds, bogs, and several large swamps.

The closest community was Kokadjo where Jon rented a house for the crew of four men, himself, and Carl for the duration of the summer. The isolated town was on the edge of the vast Maine North Woods. Jon was hopeful that he could complete the field work before heavy snows blanketed the area. He planned to use the winter months to plot the huge mosaic they had already documented. Two of the field crew and Carl would be returning to school at the end of August.

Jon was leaving the project in Carl's hands while he attended a two week summer training session at Fort Drum, New York, with the National Guard infantry company at Sanford. He left Kokadjo in mid-July to return to Wells to plan the housing, feeding and training of the company at Fort Drum. They left the Sanford Armory in a convoy of World War Two vintage two-and-a-half-ton GMC Army trucks. His command vehicle was a Dodge weapons carrier with a quad fifty-caliber machine gun mount and a radio capable of reaching several miles.

The convoy arrived at Fort Drum with a minimum of breakdowns with the ten-year-old equipment. The trip had taken over twelve hours. Jon had ordered several gallons of coffee and donuts to be made available at three-hour intervals. The troops arrived at their tented bivouac area in good spirits but were most anxious to climb out of their hard-riding vehicles. Jon insisted that the officers in the company were to stay with the men in the tents. Better quarters were available to the officers. Rank does have its privileges, but he also knew that the unit maintained a better level of morale when the officers shared the same field equipment. He understood the psyche of the foot soldier better than most officers because of his service as a sergeant in two wars.

Some officers led by authority. Jon did so by example, insisting on being at the front at all times. His respect for the American soldier was sincere and deeply ingrained. He had seen first-hand what they were capable of doing in combat. Respect that comes from the top down through the ranks is always reciprocated by the troops. Jon's record in combat was appreciated by the relatively young men in the National Guard Company.

Jon immediately met with the staff at the fort to review plans for the next two weeks. Several companies from New Hampshire, Maine, Vermont, and New York were to be grouped together to form a division and they were to function as an ad hoc infantry division, assaulting enemy fortifications. Jon was informed that he would be immediately provided with the schedule of events and the code names to be used for the various units involved. The individual companies were grouped into three regiments, but the companies were to perform in the field under their own officers who would issue orders with details answering what, when, where, and how. They were also expected to lead them through the planned maneuvers.

Jon left the headquarters building pleased with the exercises planned for them. He shared a tent with Lieutenant Nick Hall, his executive officer. They reviewed what was ahead of them once they were settled in.

"The men will be glad to get back home after this training period. This schedule will push them to the limit." Lieutenant Hall whistled at the outline distributed to all officers.

"Hard training makes actual combat easier, Nick. The men know that and expect to be tested to the limit. That's what they signed up for, and we don't want to disappoint them," Jon had replied. Training should duplicate combat as much as possible.

That night Jon stretched out on his Army cot and thought about Carl and Ashley back in Maine. The trip through Vermont and into Albany, New York, brought back memories of Jill. He had never completely forgotten her. After two years of pain and suffering, echoes from the past still lingered. It was the most difficult two years of his life. He felt an acute sense of sadness and anxiety when they had passed over Route 9 and the Hudson River north of Albany.

Maintaining the secrets from Carl and Ashley was the most trying aspect of all. Several times he had almost lost control and spoke the truth when either of them talked about their mother. They had placed her on a pedestal, and it was hard for him to support their adoration to her memory and their yearning for her touch. The hurt eventually lessened, but the anger never left him. It was as strong today as it was two years ago when he discovered the illicit affair between Jill and Lauren Hopkins.

Her duplicity and the fact that he never once perceived what was actually taking place made him angry for being so blind and stupid. It had hardened him, and that bothered Ashley and Carl the most. They had seen a change in their father over the past two years. He never talked about her or mentioned some special moment with her that had sustained him during two wars. Instead, he harbored a seething hatred for her playing him for the fool that he was. He still searched in vain for "why?" His God denied him that relief.

Six months after Jill's funeral, Jon attended an alumni reunion at the high school auditorium. He had described her accident to friends and classmates over and over to the point where he was about to leave the celebration. Joan Adams had been a close friend to both Jill and Jon. She saw his discomfort and sat beside him.

"I know this is a difficult time for you, Jon. I think everyone can understand that. It's been over ten years since I received word of Ben's death, and these gatherings are still painful. We did have some good times together, didn't we?"

"I miss Ben, too," Jon replied. Joan had always been a good friend, and he was not surprised that Ben's memory was still alive and meaningful. "Ben was a lucky guy, Joan. I often think of the times when we went hunting together and going deep sea fishing with his father on their lobster boat."

"It's nice when we can recall pleasant times. They enrich our lives. Ever since Jill's funeral I've seen a different you, my dear friend. Sadness and yearning for a loved one is normal and appropriate. I apologize for what I'm going to say, Jon, but I've seen a bitterer person than I've known since we were in the first grade. Those of us who cherish your friendship care. Forgive me, but I had to tell you the truth."

Jon took her hands in his. She knew him well enough to distinguish mourning a loss and being angry. "I can always accept the truth from a friend. You're a perceptive person, Joan. If you see bitterness as you call it, maybe it's because I won't be able to share the dreams Jill and I had planned for the future now that the kids are out of high school. Maybe I'm just being selfish and only thinking of myself. If I've alarmed you, I'm sorry. Give me some time, Joan."

She smiled and squeezed his hand. The orchestra was playing an old favorite, *Tennessee Waltz*. "Will you dance this one with me?"

"It's my pleasure. Thanks for caring enough to be honest with me."

From that evening on, Jon began to improve. He vividly recalled how Joan had handled the death of her beloved husband in the war. She had been saddened and was a forlorn, lonely person for a long time, but she never felt sorry for herself. She worshipped Ben's memory without making him out to be a God, which he was not. Carl and Ashley both witnessed a change in their father. His brooding moodiness had worried them, too.

While Jon was at Fort Drum, he called Carl often to check on the progress of the job, and was pleased that things were going smoothly. One of the men got into a nest of yellow jackets that bit him fifteen times, making him momentarily lose consciousness. They carried him out of the forest and quickly drove him to the Greenville Hospital. They had given him some histamine cold medicine to control the swelling. The next day he was back on the job. Jon joked that he expected to find Carl full of questions. Instead he was confident of continuing the job as Jon had wanted. Carl seemed to be enjoying himself.

Jon laughed with his son and said, "Every older person is shocked when they find that they can be replaced by young, competent men who have had less experience, but make up for the deficiency with enthusiasm. I'm pleased, Son. I'll see you as soon as we're finished here. When you finish your ROTC classes, you'll be attending a training base like Fort Drum. I love you, Son. Take care of yourself."

The company had just returned to camp after a grueling day in the field, and the men were looking forward to some leisure time. Movies were shown every night at the base theatre, and the ever popular USO always provided entertainment and good food. Several of the officers from the division were going into Watertown, New York, for an evening of relaxation. Jon and Lieutenant Nick Hall joined them. Those who knew the area had picked a popular steakhouse restaurant and had reserved several tables for the officers.

Jon and Lieutenant Hall selected a table with two other officers from a New York regiment. Lt. Hall had met both of them and introduced Jon. "Gentlemen, this is our New Hampshire company commander, Captain Jon Burke. Captain, this young man on my right is Second Lieutenant Alfred Hopkins. Captain Truman Morehouse is on my left of the Lieutenant. As you can already tell by his ribbons, Captain Burke is a highly decorated veteran of two wars."

The young Lieutenant Hopkins looked familiar to Jon the moment they entered the dining room. His father was Lauren Hopkins! "I'm glad to meet you, Captain Morehouse, and you, too, Lieutenant Hopkins. I have a son in school a little younger than you. He's enrolled in ROTC." Jon extended his hand to the two officers. Lieutenant Hopkins recognized Jon. Their eyes met, and instantly, old memories clouded the enthusiasm that had brought them out from the fort for an evening of relaxation.

Lieutenant Hopkins was speechless and uttered, "I'm glad to meet you, Captain."

Morehouse and Hall saw the awkwardness of the meeting of the two men. Captain Morehouse added, "Have you two met before?" The question broke the chill in the room.

Jon saw Lieutenant Hopkins lose control and left his seat to embrace the young officer. It was a poignant moment for all of the men.

"Gentlemen," explained Jon in a strained voice. "Alfred and I share a heavy burden that is not easy to hide. Alfred's father and my wife were killed in a tragic auto accident two years ago. They were both engineers who had worked together on several projects as independent consultants. The last time I saw this young officer was in Glens Falls where he was studying the wrecked Nash the two were riding in. My heart went out to you at that time, but I was too consumed by my own grief to be of any help. If my presence continues to bring back painful memories, I'll excuse myself. I have no desire to be a source of discomfort to you, Lieutenant."

Alfred, released from the embrace, shook Jon's hand. "No, please don't excuse yourself, Captain. I was caught off guard, and echoes from the past overwhelmed me. I'm okay, Sir. I do not want to cause a scene with a superior officer. Please, share our table with us."

"Son, you're a credit to the uniform. The Army needs young men like you. I understand that you have an Army tradition in your family. I wish you the best of luck," replied Jon, reaching for his wine glass. "I propose a toast to all the young officers who have the grave responsibility of leading men in combat. May the grace of God guide their footsteps in the future."

The four raised their glasses in a toast. For the rest of the evening, they discussed the maneuvers scheduled for the next week at Fort Drum. The younger officers at the table were awed by the rows of ribbons on Jon's chest and his vast experience in World War Two and Korea. He had earned a Distinguished Service Cross, two Silver Stars, one Bronze Star, and a Purple Heart. His Combat Infantry Badge was worn above all the other ribbons. Jon had also earned a battlefield commission, the ultimate test of leadership skills. His easy-going and unassuming air earned him the respect of the men in his command. Lieutenant Hall held him on a pedestal as the officer he would most like to emulate.

Just as they were completing their steaks, two young ladies, who were obviously twins, arrived at the table unannounced.

Alfred rose to greet them. "Wow, what a nice surprise." He turned to the officers around the table and announced, "Gentlemen, these are my twin sisters, Elaine and Eileen."

The evening was full of unusual expectations for Jon. He recalled that Mrs. Hopkins had mentioned twin girls, but he had not given it any thought. Alfred proudly introduced them to everyone at the table who graciously made room for the ladies to join them. Lieutenant Hall was quick to borrow two additional chairs from an adjoining table. When Jon's last name was mentioned, the two girls looked at him with searching eyes, lingering on the ribbons on his chest.

Jon thought to himself, "They know who I am."

Alfred was proud to tell them that the twins were attending nursing school and planned to join the Army Nurse Corps.

Jon was quick to add, "The Army nurse is the most respected individual in the entire U.S. Army. They've earned that cherished position by displaying courage, compassion, and dedication above and beyond. I salute your plans for the future, ladies."

"Thank you, Captain Burke." They replied in unison.

Elaine, who appeared to be the most talkative of the two, turned to Alfred. "Al, we have another surprise for you. Mother is visiting with some elderly friends of the family who live in the area. She thought we might all go to a movie or something."

Hall and Morehouse urged Alfred to go with his sisters. He looked at Jon with some hesitation. "I don't want to spoil a good evening with you gentlemen."

"Lieutenant Hopkins," Jon was quick to reply, "You go and enjoy yourself with your family. They were very considerate of their brother, and please say hello to your mother for me. I think I'll return to base and have a small nightcap at the Officers' Club before turning in for the evening. My company has worked my tail of this week. Enjoy the visit with your family, Lieutenant."

"Thanks, guys," Alfred said, leaving the restaurant with his sisters.

Lieutenant Hall followed the twins out through the door. "If he had asked, I would have gladly joined him. They are two attractive young ladies."

"That they are," Jon agreed. "Well, you guys can enjoy a night on the town. Us older men have got to get our beauty sleep. I'll see you when you return to base."

Jon jumped on an Army bus that ran shuttle services between Watertown and the base. He immediately checked regimental headquarters to make sure everything was under control. The young lieutenant that had the duty as officer of the day was sitting at a desk reading a paperback book. He spotted Jon in the doorway. "This place is like a schoolroom after the bell has rung. Ninety percent of the men are either at the activity center or Watertown. Everything is under control, Captain Burke."

"Thanks, Lieutenant. I'm gonna stop at the Officer's Club before turning in. That book you're reading, *Profiles in Courage*, is a good one. I've read it twice. Good night, Lieutenant."

"Good night, Sir."

The Officers' Clubs on most military installations are busy places after hours, and Fort Drum was no exception. Jon was not hungry but he did want a cup or two of coffee. Jill used to complain that it would keep him awake at night. It never did; instead, it seemed to relax him more than stimulate him. He got a coffee at the serving table and took a seat with two colonels he knew from the Korean War.

They spent an hour or more discussing how the Army had changed since the Korean ceasefire. Jon had given serious thought to rejoining the active Army since Jill was no longer a part of his life. His life seemed empty, and he was weary trying to fill each day with activity. He knew he had to make a living to support him and Carl, but it was not the same. The two colonels excused themselves and left him alone in the dining room.

He went to the serving table to get another cup of coffee and a piece of custard pie and returned to his table. He had noticed a woman standing in the doorway of the foyer. She was adjusting her eyes to the dim lights. He thought nothing of it. Most officers came with their wives or sweethearts for a little relaxation after taps. He stirred two spoons of sugar in his coffee and saw the woman approaching his table.

She announced herself in a low voice. "Captain Burke, I hope I'm not interrupting your evening. I heard that you were here, and I had some questions to ask you."

Jon looked closer at the lady dressed in a pair of green slacks and a dark green blazer with a light tan beret sitting at a rakish angle on her head. It was Amber Hopkins!

Chapter Eight

"Please take a seat, Mrs. Hopkins. You're not interrupting me. I'm enjoying a cup of coffee and a delicious piece of custard pie. May I get you a serving?"

"It's been a long time since I had coffee and pie at this time of the evening," she said, taking a seat. "It smells tempting. Yes, Captain, I'd like that. Thank you for asking."

"I'll be right back, Ma'am."

He returned to the table with pie ala mode and coffee with cream and sugar on a tray. He smiled, placing it in front of her. "It'll either make you sleep better or keep you up most of the night."

"It looks delicious. I am hungry."

She seemed to be a lot more at ease and rested than the last time he had met her two years ago at Lake George. "I was surprised to learn that your son, Lieutenant Hopkins, was in one of the New York units. He's a fine young man and has the makings of being a fine officer. My son, Carl, is a couple of years younger than Alfred. He's also considering a career in the Army. I also met your twin daughters earlier this evening. They're lovely ladies."

"Yes," she replied, stirring her coffee. "Al told me that he had met you. He was impressed by the ribbons you wear. I recognize what they represent."

She was still uneasy in his presence. He knew how difficult it was to live with the ugly flashbacks. Once she sat down at the table with him, the same old feelings of helplessness and anger returned with equal vigor. He suspected it was the same with her.

"After I talked with the children, I thought it was important for me to ask if you were successful in sheltering the truth from them. I hate myself for revisiting old wounds, but the children keep asking me why your wife, Jill, was with my Lauren at such

51

a time in the morning. That part has been difficult, especially with the twins. I think Al has figured it out and remains silent..."

He understood what she was saying and wondered if they had been right in trying to shelter the children. The truth would be hurtful, but it would get it over with once and for all, and the healing could begin from that moment. As it was now, Jon and Amber carried the burden of guilt in not being open and forthright. It was becoming cumbersome.

She continued, "I still have questions in search of answers, Captain. Perhaps we should have laid out the whole ugly scene. The anger still lingers with no resolution in sight. What questions do you still have?"

"That's easy," he replied. "Where did the clothes Jill was wearing at the time of the accident come from? She never, I repeat, never, owned clothes so suggestive and revealing. And of course, the most dominant question of all remains like a festering wound. What did I do or fail to do that triggered such deception from Jill? She never revealed that side of her makeup to me...never. Was I blind and stupid so that she played me for a backwoods chump? I don't know. There's no logical answer. All of the children are intelligent and perceptive people who have seen through our charade. If I was in their shoes, I'd do a little independent checking of the facts to satisfy my curiosity. That they may have done so should not surprise us, Mrs. Hopkins."

She sipped her coffee and looked away from him to hide the tears in her eyes. "It's been two years, and every day I carry the same hurt and frustration in search of the same answers. I've developed an intense hatred towards your wife and my husband. I can't help it. There has to be an end to this kind of a life...I... I can't plan anything. The future is clouded by the darkness that has ruled my life since the accident.

"I better understand now how an alcoholic can use the stuff to escape the pain of reality. I've tried a few times, but I hate liquor. That route is not an answer for me... I apologize, Captain, for carrying on so," she nervously exclaimed.

Jon reached across the table and took her hands in his. "We've been traveling down that same road. I understand, and I also have feelings of contempt. I'm glad you felt strong enough to approach me and talk about our mutual problem. It's just not fair for us, or for the kids. It's time for God to look upon our situation and grant us some element of peace. We've paid a high enough price for our spouses' infidelity. Be strong, ma'am. We can't give up. We owe that to ourselves and to the kids."

She pulled her hands from his and blew her nose and wiped away the tears forming in her eyes. "I can't tell you how comforting it is to talk about things. I grew up as an Army brat who liked plain talk. It was a way of life in our family. Not being able to discuss it has been the hardest part of all. I could share it with some of my closest friends, but I'm ashamed that this has come about because of some deficiency on my part."

"Perhaps I've been less troubled because my daughter's husband went to New York to get Jill's car. We made a pact to keep it quiet. That has helped a lot. Hal is like a son to me, so the burden has not been as heavy for me as it has for you, Mrs. Hopkins."

"Would you consider me bold if I suggest that we call each other by our first names? Captain and Mrs. seem too formal for our situation," she asked, tasting her pie.

"I've been thinking the same thing, so Amber it is for me. That's a pretty name," he replied with a smile.

She looked at him with her sad eyes and said, "The way you spell your name, Jon, is unique. Being here in the Officers' Club at Fort Drum is like coming home for me. My father had duty here often over the years. A lot of old friends have settled in this region. It's a beautiful part of New York State. Most people associate the state as being like the city of New York. The people up here are wonderful. I'm so glad I came with the twins to see Al. When they told me about you, I felt an urge to discuss our common problem again. Thank you for being so helpful. I was afraid I was going to make a fool of myself again. Lately I've felt trapped with no place to escape. These past two years have been a long journey, but you already know that."

"What do you say if we spend the rest of the evening not talking about things we have no way of controlling? I've started a large survey project in northern Maine that's kind of exciting. Work has been good therapy for me. My relationship with the wonderful gang at the local National Guard unit has also helped a lot. Right after the accident, I joined the Guard."

"Instead of looking forward," Amber began, slowly feeling more comfortable with the conversation, "I've been recalling memories of a wonderful childhood. My relationship with my mother was very warm and full. Father was a little firm, but I loved him dearly for his compassion. He had the ability to create something positive out of chaos. He was the peacemaker in the family. My older brother died unexpectedly playing baseball in high school. The tragedy helped to bring the family closer together. Suddenly little differences seemed less significant, and we attended church more often. Faith really helped. I pray for that level of peace and comfort that comes from faith and am making an earnest effort to recapture it. My father led the family to that source of strength that gives meaning to life."

"Where did your father go to school?" Jon asked, interested in a general officer who had made a career in the Army.

"He was a West Point graduate who served in the Mexican campaign and the two world wars. My only brother, Richard, had already been selected for West Point when he died of a heart attack. My father was a very strong man who shared his grief and disappointment with no one. I understand his pain now better than ever."

"Most of my childhood and adult life involved Jill. It's difficult to look back at a time when she was not a part of my daily life. I apologize for bringing it up, but it's hard to look back and not see her in the picture…"

Amber understood his dilemma. "You had a relationship with Jill that was the opposite of mine with Lauren. He was a young football player at college and was popular with the girls. I was one who felt lucky if he noticed me. I was more shy and reserved back then. We dated a few times, and he swept me off my feet. We eventually married because I was pregnant… He wanted me to get an abortion, but I refused. My father had a talk with him, and soon after that we were married. My father never told me what took place between them, but from that time, Lauren avoided my father as much as possible. My father was probably the only person he was afraid of. I can imagine what happened between them. Neither of them divulged their secret. You had a loving and caring relationship with Jill; I envy you for that."

"That may be true. Possibly it made it easier for Jill to deceive me. I'm still a simple country bumpkin," declared Jon, surprised that he could talk so candidly about her.

"Don't sell yourself short, Jon. Those ribbons on your uniform tell the world a lot about you," she quickly replied. "I'm glad that I had the chance to visit with you like this. I was having trouble keeping all of the sordid details to myself. You and I share a secret that could be emotionally damaging to the children. They deserve better legacies from our deceased."

"I never thought of it that way. You're correct. My son Carl is running a large job for me while I'm away. I may find that he's doing such a fine job that it makes me obsolete," he laughed.

Amber picked up on his self-deprecating attitude. "I'm glad for you. We do have to climb out of this cesspool we've been thrown into, or we'll drown in depravity. As for me, I'm determined to continue researching a number of historic events that have fascinated me for a long, long time."

"I remember you telling me you majored in history. I've been a student of military history all of my life. It was impossible to avoid it in the Army. I'm glad for you. We need to follow whatever captures our interest. I've always been interested with the significance of the Hudson River-Lake Champlain corridor in our early nation-building-efforts during the French and Indian War and the Revolutionary War."

"That was one of the main reasons I wanted to settle in the Albany area. It has a rich legacy for all Americans," she explained with enthusiasm. "Sitting here talking like this reminds me of one project, the courageous trek through the Maine wilderness by Benedict Arnold, that has received very little scholarship. It was early in the Revolution and during the dead of winter. He failed to capture Quebec, but that does not diminish the heroic effort that took place."

"I know that area quite well," Jon added. "One of my first survey jobs was to relocate and document the boundaries of Fort Halifax and Fort Western on the Kennebec River. I worked for the Maine Historical Society in Augusta. If and when you're ready to study the area firsthand, I'll be glad to help where I can."

"I'll remember your generous offer, Jon," she replied, getting up to return the coffee cup and plates to the serving area. "It's getting late. The fort commander reserved quarters for us at the Hospitality Center. I plan to visit Alfred and return to Albany with the twins."

"How did you get to the Officers' Club?" he asked.

"An old friend dropped me off. Al took the Buick for the evening and promised to pick me up."

"May I offer you a ride back to the center? I have the company Jeep outside. Rank has its privileges," he smiled.

"I accept your offer, Jon. Thank you for sharing the evening with depressing talk. It has been refreshing to vent some of the grief and to know that I'm not alone with the sorrow. I've been selfish and have only thought of myself."

Jon paid for their tab and escorted her out to the Jeep with a cloth top.

"It's a couple of miles back to the Hospitality Center. Jeeps can be cool at night. May I offer my summer tunic and place it over your shoulders? I'll be fine the way I am."

"Thank you. I hadn't thought of that. It will feel good," she said, accepting his hand getting into the Jeep.

He retrieved the tunic from the rear seat of the Jeep and draped it over her shoulders.

"Thank you," she said, fastening one button of the tunic to keep it from falling off. "It's been a long time since I rode in a Jeep."

"I had a Jeep pickup truck for several years. It was a dependable vehicle. I traded it in on my Studebaker pickup which I like very much."

He started the Jeep and turned around, heading back to the command center of the fort. This had been a pleasant evening with Amber. He had smiled and even laughed a few times. It had helped to release some of the pressure that was always present since the accident. He also had the feeling that it had helped the lady beside him. For the first time since the tragedy, he saw a chance for him to gain some resemblance of a normal life. He had to shed the shackles of bondage. The anger that he carried was becoming too heavy a burden for him. He pulled to a stop at the Base Hospitality Center and got out to help Amber from the Jeep.

"I've enjoyed our conversation this evening, Amber. I needed a chance to talk."

"Our talk has helped me to put this chapter of my life to rest," she said, accepting his helping hand. "Thanks for the ride, Jon Burke." She quickly embraced him and disappeared into the building.

Chapter Nine

The National Guard companies were kept busy in the field, rain or shine, for the duration of the second week of training. Their battalion commander took sick, and Jon filled in as acting commander while turning over his Sanford Company to Lieutenant Hall.

Upon completion of the training period, the ad hoc division passed in review before a stand filled with guests and brass. Jon recognized Amber and the twins who sat on each side of her. All of the New York units were leaving immediately after the parade. Jon held the Sanford Company at their quarters until the next morning when they were scheduled to leave, first thing in the morning, so that they could make the trip home in one day.

Jon and Lieutenant Hall elected to eat breakfast at the Officers' Club which was less crowded that time in the morning. They went through the line selecting French toast, bacon, and coffee. They turned to take a seat in the dining hall and saw Amber, Alfred, and the twins sitting near the serving tables.

Lieutenant Hall recognized the twins. "Shall we join them, Jon?" he asked.

Jon saw Amber motion that there was room at their table. "Sure, Nick. Why not? You know the twins." Jon sat at the end of the long table between Eileen and Amber and was introduced to the twins again.

"I saw all of you at the reviewing stand. You must be proud of your son, Mrs. Hopkins. It's nice to see you again, Lieutenant. I remembered the names of the twins, but will have trouble telling which is Eileen or Elaine," he smiled.

"Don't feel bad, Captain. I can't either," Lieutenant Hopkins remarked, laughing out loud. "Sometimes they dress the same and trade places just to confuse us. Mother can't be fooled, but I can on a regular basis."

The twins laughed playfully with their brother. Jon thought it was nice to experience the friendly family banter. For a moment he was aware of the twins' intense study of him, and he was uncomfortable. He assumed that they were mentally questioning why his wife, Jill, was alone with their father so early in the morning at the time of the crash. He did not blame them. He was curious if they had discovered the truth.

Lieutenant Hall and Jon were anxious to leave. They had much to do before leaving in the morning. With that they said their good-byes and shook hands with everyone at the table. Jon was glad to be heading home.

Fourteen hours later, Jon was supervising the storage of the equipment at the Sanford armory. He quickly jumped in his Studebaker pickup, relieved to be home. It was about eight o'clock in the evening when he turned into his driveway and noticed Ashley's Nash Rambler in the yard. The kitchen light was on. He had called Ashley and Hal from Newburgh, New York, that they were on their way home. Ashley had seen him park his truck and met her father at the door.

He gave her a warm hug and closed the door behind him. She had a sober look on her face. "What's the matter, Ashley?"

She walked to his desk in the office off the kitchen. "I came over to make sure the house was in order for your homecoming, Dad. I cleaned up the dishes you left in the sink," she cried, avoiding his penetrating eyes.

"I did leave in a hurry," he quickly exclaimed.

"I was dusting in your office and noticed this letter from the coroner's office at Glens Falls. The autopsy report stated that mother died of trauma to her head and chest when she was thrown against the windshield," Ashley stated with a shaky voice.

"Yes, I've already told you that, Ashley."

"I know, but then I turned to the back of the page and read that a simple test performed on all accidental deaths showed that she had fresh semen in her vagina…"

Jon knew what was wrong. She had discovered his cover-up. "That's the truth, dear daughter," he answered.

Ashley exploded with anger and pain. "Do you realize what that simple statement tells us, Dad? Mother was with another man prior to the accident," she screamed, unable to control herself.

Jon grabbed Ashley and held her close to him. She cried for several minutes in his protective arms and pulled away from his embrace. "Why didn't you tell Carl and me, Dad?"

"I kept the secret to myself to shield you and your brother from the pain and anger you're now experiencing. Honest, dear daughter, I was only thinking of you kids. The monstrous deception has just about driven me crazy these past two years. Sharing it with you two would never have accomplished anything except to hurt you. I meant to destroy that damned report! I'm so sorry, Ashley, I really am. That report validated my original impression. Nothing made any sense, except that she had known this man for a period of time. How could she? Why? Why? I thought I had put it to rest. Now you've got to live with the truth. Hal knew, Ashley. I made him promise not to divulge our secret."

"I had a feeling Hal was keeping something from me," she cried, wiping the tears from her eyes.

"I insisted, Ashley. No one had tried to protect you more than your husband. Trust me, Honey, we were only concerned for you and Carl. You two are all I've got now, and I'd do anything to keep you from getting hurt. Hal feels the same."

For the past two years, Jon had carried the hurt close to his heart. Each day he was getting stronger. His talks with Amber had helped a lot. Now his dear Ashley was tainted by the truth and the conspiracy to shelter her. Suddenly he was weary, and that old feeling of helplessness haunted him.

Ashley saw the lines about her father's mouth and eyes. She was hurt and dismayed by the discovery, but her gentle father had carried the information alone for two years. Now she better understood the horror and far-away-look she had often seen in his eyes. Neither she nor Carl could comfort him. The fact that her mother had created such havoc on a man who loved and cherished her for years filled Ashley with a terrible loathing for the act of deception. She embraced him. "I'm sorry to have caused such a scene, Dad. Mom was blessed with the wonderful love of a good man. God will punish her for that. I pray that God will also comfort you and allow you to put this sordid affair behind you."

The embrace unleashed the tears bursting for release. Ashley's discovery of the truth had lifted the burden he had carried ever since the accident. Now that she knew, the family could put the past where it belonged and embrace the future. Amidst all the sadness Jill's death had produced, it had drawn Jon closer than ever to his children. He had that to be thankful for.

That evening, after Ashley left, he experienced a catharsis that cleansed his soul and eased the grief that had dominated his life for two years. He sat on the sofa in the living room and prayed for the strength to build a new life free of the anguish and sorrow that had blanketed his family. He had two wonderful children, a granddaughter he adored, and a son-in-law that had become a close friend. For those gifts he was thankful.

That next morning, he was up early before dawn and was eager to see how Carl was doing on the survey job. After shaving, showering, and closing up the house, Jon climbed into his truck. The lawn needed mowing, he smiled to himself. He bet that Hal would mow it by the time he and Carl returned. His Ashley had chosen well.

Jon stopped at Cozy Corner, a small café on Route One towards Kennebunk that was a popular eating spot. He saw Joan Adams' Chevrolet coupe in the parking lot. He entered the restaurant and saw her in a booth close to the entrance. She recognized him and motioned for him to join her.

"You're up early, Joan," he said, taking a seat across the table from her.

"I resigned from the York Hospital and accepted a job at a convalescent home in Kennebunkport. It's a lot closer for me to travel, and I can have most weekends off," she told him. "How was your training excursion at Fort Drum?"

"The best we've had in a long time. Carl took over the work project for me while I was away. I'm on my way to Kokadjo. I called him every day to see how he was getting along. I may find that I'm not needed," he grinned.

She noticed the softer lines around his mouth and his deep-set eyes. The smile was a lot like the Jon Burke she had known all her life. She returned his smile. "I'm not surprised. He's a fine young man a lot like his father."

He ordered scrambled eggs, English muffins and coffee and studied Joan. She had aged gracefully. They were the same age. She wore her hair cut short slightly below her ears and was wearing a white nurse uniform. He never thought of her as being beautiful or showy like Jill, yet there was something wholesome about her. She projected an air of dignity and decency that defined her as well as a willingness to take on the world. She had raised a son, paid off a house she and Ben had purchased before the war, and was first in line to help where she was needed in the small community. Life had not been easy for her, yet she never complained. She was a good friend who never asked for anything for herself. He admired her for that and the way she met life's challenges head on.

"You're looking good, Jon. It's nice to see you smile again," she said, sipping her coffee.

He acknowledged her remark with another smile. "I'm lucky to have a friend like you, Joan. I've been acting a little selfish. When I see how you handled Ben's death and faced the world alone, I'm ashamed of my self-pity."

"Oh, I've had my days when it would have been easy to run away from it all, Jon. I always envied you and Jill."

He almost shared his secret with her and controlled his response. "Yes, I was lucky. What do you say if you and I go out for a movie somewhere and have a good meal someone else has prepared? I can be back from Kokadjo most weekends."

"Are you asking me for a date, Jon?"

"Of course I am. You and I go back a long ways. It would be fun, and I'd be proud to be with you."

Joan's eyes moistened, and she avoided his inquiring glance. "I'd like that, Jon. I'm forty-five years old with more gray hair than brown."

"You're the same age as me," he said forcefully. "And furthermore, you're still an attractive woman with more grit than anyone I know. I was afraid you'd refuse, and I'd be embarrassed," he replied, pleased with her answer.

"Jon Burke, you've made my day," she exclaimed, getting ready to leave. "I can honestly tell you that there have been requests from several men for a date. I refuse most of them. Before Ben and I married, I carried a long-standing crush on you. I envied Jill. I must warn you, Jon. I'm not Jill, and I could

61

never be like Jill, and it would be unfair to her memory and to me if you expect a replacement for her in your life."

Her answer was typical of what he expected of her. "Joan, I could never compare you to Jill. Trust me, dear friend, that will never happen. You know, I feel like a kid on his first date. I'll look forward to the weekend. Thanks."

She got up to leave and kissed him on the cheek. "Thanks for asking, Jon. I'll be waiting for your call."

He waved to her through the window as she turned her coupe toward the road to Kennebunkport.

Jon drove nonstop from Wells to Greenville where he stopped to fill the truck's gas tank. The route further north was void of any filling stations. He grabbed a pocketful of candy bars and left for the final leg of his trip.

The long drive gave him a chance to review where he had been. The past two years had been tumultuous and uncertain. He had gone through each day much like a robot. He worked because he needed the money. Slowly his outlook for the future was more positive. The day he had signed for the large survey contract was eventful, and his spirits rose afterwards. Everyone was telling him that life goes on, but he had to discover that for himself. He was more ready to take on the world now than he was a year ago. That was progress. Asking Joan for a date was a milestone for him. A year ago it would never have crossed his mind. Memories of Jill had filled his life.

The house that he had rented at Kokadjo was really a summer cottage on First Roach Pond. The plot of land they were surveying was located north of First Roach Pond, south of Third Roach pond, and extended easterly to the Piscataquis-Penobscot County line, including all of Second Roach Pond. He had reconnoitered the area and had it photographed from the air. Aerial photos would be a lot of help in delineating different features on the land. It also was a time saver in plotting contour lines. The technology since World War Two had been expanded in the science of aerial photography.

The same image on the ground photographed from different locations made it possible for a person to use a mirror stereoscope that show images in the third dimension. It was possible to compute elevations and to superimpose contour lines on the terrain without having to do a large amount of field measurements. Carl had been trained to use the new technology in his forestry courses. It saved them days of field work and was accurate enough to delineate the drainage patterns of watersheds.

When Jon drove into the driveway of the cottage, he saw all five men swimming in the pond. He hailed Carl and carried into the cottage a large box of groceries. Everyone who has ever visited the Maine woods has experienced a profound increase of appetite. Even food not normally enjoyed tasted good. Jon was always prepared with a statewide favorite, baked beans. It was a North Woods staple food. The men ate some at every meal.

Carl climbed out of the water, grabbing a towel to dry himself. "We expected you this afternoon, Dad. How did the training session go?"

"It was great," he explained. "The men are anxious to go home though. Now, how did you make out, Son?"

Carl was prepared for the question and guided his father to the large map plotted on two large pieces of plywood on the living room wall. They jokingly called it their war room. Carl had plotted all of the field data completed to-date. Contour lines at ten-foot intervals were added as they progressed. Several complete watersheds had already been documented. Carl told his father that he and the crew had decided to spend as many hours in the field each day as was possible. Then they could plot the field data on rainy days, therefore speeding up the operation.

"We can complete this project in two more weeks, Dad, weather permitting," Carl proudly predicted.

"That's great, Son. I'm pleased with the progress you've made without me," Jon replied, examining the latest additions to the map in progress. "Your forestry training is beginning to show, Carl. You've done well."

That evening, after supper dishes had been washed and dried, Jon mentioned something he had been thinking about for a while. "What do you say if you and I take a day and climb Mount Katahdin? The men will want to go home for the weekend. I've always been fascinated by the mountain. It stands like a giant sentinel in the northern forest. We can drive up to Rippogenus Dam and then drive to Baxter State Park from the west and sleep overnight in one of their Adirondack shelters. That way we could tackle the mountain early in the morning when we're fresh."

"That sounds great to me," Carl answered. He was pleased to see a more positive and energetic attitude in his father. "I climbed Mount Chocorua in the White Mountains with some of my forestry friends. We also did Mount Monadnock in Jaffrey, New Hampshire. That was an easy climb up and down in one day. Boston was so visible that we could actually see people through the windows in some of the tall buildings with our binoculars. I've been impressed with Katahdin ever since we started this project. It should be a fun trip, Dad. Why don't we aim for next weekend, weather permitting?"

"I have an appointment for this weekend at home," Jon told his son without explaining about Joan. "Since you and the men have done so well, why don't we give them a long weekend off, and you and I could tackle the mountain Friday morning? We could drive to the shelter Thursday afternoon after work."

"The men will like that, Dad."

Jon embraced his son. "You may have to help me over some of the rough spots," he joked.

Chapter Ten

The four men eagerly left for home, leaving Jon and Carl time to climb Mount Katahdin before going back to Wells for the weekend. Jon left for Greenville to use the telephone to confirm his date with Joan.

She answered the phone on the first ring. "Hello."

"Hi, Joan. This is Jon. I'm calling to confirm our date for this weekend."

"Oh, Jon, I'm so glad you called," she replied. "I just found out that one of the nurses at the home came down sick, and I have to fill in for her. I hope you're not disappointed. I know that I am, but I can firmly promise that the following weekend will be open for me."

He told her about his plan to climb Katahdin with Carl. "I'll feel guilty with you working extra shifts, but duty calls. I'll stay up here for now and will definitely be in Wells next weekend. Carl and I will leave to stay in a shelter the night before we do the climb to Baxter Peak. It should be fun."

"I'm so glad to hear you talk like that, Jon. You and Carl enjoy yourselves. I've heard that it's a beautiful view from the top. I'll be looking forward to next weekend. Be careful now."

Things worked out well for everybody. Carl was anxious to attack the mountain. They loaded up the Studebaker pickup and headed for one of the most scenic drives in the state of Maine.

The main road north from Greenville was gravel and was located on private land holdings of the Great Northern Paper Company. They stopped at the large lake created by the Ripogenus Dam. Several watersheds drained into the large reservoir, making it a natural location to divert pulpwood through a large sluiceway at the northern end of the dam to the paper mills at Millinocket. Water level was maintained by powerful gear-driven steel gates. The drop in elevation of the sluiceway from the reservoir was ten to twenty feet. The wood plummeted through the gate at a rapid speed, giving it momentum to travel several miles to the mill.

Twenty miles southeast of the dam, Jon pulled the truck into the main entrance road to Baxter State Park where they registered themselves and filled out an itinerary of their hike the next day. The ranger on duty checked to see that they were properly equipped for the trail hikes they had outlined. They also paid the required fees for the use of the park and the Adirondack shelter at the campground. There were several empty shelters. They parked and selected one beside the bubbling brook known as Katahdin Stream. The sun had just dropped out of sight of the massive peaks in the White Mountains of New Hampshire.

The Baxter State Park was a gift from Governor Percival P. Baxter who had used his wealth to purchase vast tracts of land in northern Maine. He gave it to the people with the understanding that it be maintained as "Forever Wild." His wish of keeping it natural is treated as a strict order. He said: "The works of man are short-lived. Monuments decay, buildings crumble, and wealth vanishes, but Katahdin in its massive grandeur will forever remain the mountain of the people of Maine. Through the ages it will stand as an inspiration to the men and women of the state." Its isolation from heavy populations has made it a favorite attraction for those who wish to break away from the stress of civilization and to enjoy one of the most primitive and beautiful wilderness experiences in the United States.

"Why don't you start a fire in the fireplace in front of the shelter, Carl? I'll roll out our sleeping bags on the floor of the shelter," Jon pointed to the fireplace. They had brought along several armfuls of dry firewood for the occasion. Even in the summertime a small fire feels good in the Maine woods.

They ate peanut butter and jelly sandwiches and drank hot tea as they sat on the edge of the floor, watching darkness envelope the wilderness. They boiled a half dozen eggs to eat on the trail the next day. They also made up several peanut butter and jelly sandwiches. Jon told Carl that he had brought along two small blocks of sharp cheddar cheese. Eggs, cheese, and sandwiches constituted their day's food for the trip. They divided it equally between their two back packs so that they did not have heavy loads to tote. Both of them included a sweater and an extra pair of socks to change into at the top of the climb. It reflected an old infantryman's attention to his feet. Now they were ready for the climb in the morning.

Carl had been observing his father since he returned from Camp Drum. He was much more at ease than he had been since the accident. He was by nature a quiet person who rarely pushed his opinions upon anyone and cherished his moments of solitude whether it was in the living room at home or the forest wilderness.

Several campers had arrived to fill most of the shelters, but Carl and his father were alone in the shelter they selected. The privacy suited Jon just fine. He was debating if this was a good time to tell Carl about his discussion with Ashley. He was fully aware that it would be a jarring revelation to his son. The issue weighed heavily on his mind ever since he left Wells. Watching the red embers in the fireplace in a serene atmosphere close to nature was as good a time and place as any other.

"Son, I have something to tell you that I've kept from you and Ashley about the accident. Your sister was at the house cleaning up for us when I arrived from the Armory. She had read the report from the Glens Falls' coroner's office stating that your mother had sexual relations shortly prior to the accident. It was obvious that it had to have been the man also killed, Lauren Hopkins. Please don't be angry at me for keeping it from you and Ashley. Now that she knows, you have that same right. Be brave, Son."

Carl sat quietly on the floor of the shelter with his feet dangling over the edge. He too was staring at the embers. Jon leaned over to place an arm around Carl. He knew that his son was processing every word he had spoken. "Are you telling me that Mother was having an affair with that man?"

Jon felt his body stiffen. "Yes, Son. I knew it was something that would hurt you kids, so I chose to keep it from you. Hal knew, and we both agreed to keep it quiet. When I got home, Ashley had already read the report and came to the correct conclusion about what had taken place."

"My God, how can I explain that to my friends?"

"No one else needs to know, Carl. I hate to burden you like this, but there isn't any good time to hear such unpleasant news," Jon added reluctantly, wondering if he had made a mistake.

Carl remained in control of his emotions better than expected. He began in a weak voice: "I have to tell you, Dad, that Ashley and I have talked a lot about the accident. We both had the feeling that something was missing. Mom being out in the early hours of the morning with a stranger was, to us, something that anyone would question. We were not strong enough to think the worst, but it was always there as a remote possibility even if neither of us dared to talk to you about it."

"I expected you two to have questions, but you never expressed them," Jon said, shaking his head.

"We did that out of respect for you, Dad. We could see that something was eating away at you. You've not been the same. You've been angry more than we've seen you sad, and that fact made us wonder if there was something we were not told. I'm glad that Ashley brought it out in the open. Now we can put it where it belongs. Mom will be punished for this betrayal. As for me, I want to remember her the way it was before the accident. I loved that person very much. The one that died in New York is a total stranger to me. Ashley will be okay, Dad, and so will I. You have to put this episode behind you. Mom is in the hands of our Maker and we should leave judgment to Him."

Jon was astounded by the maturity and wisdom of his son. He was no longer a boy, but a man who made his Dad proud. Jon embraced him and said: "What do you say if we hit the sack? I'm weary."

"So am I. Thanks for trying to shelter Ashley and me from being hurt. Sure, it's a shocker, but the truth makes it easier to accept and live with. We were as concerned for you as you were for us. Goodnight, Dad. I'm looking forward to tomorrow. Do you snore?"

Jon smiled as he climbed into the sleeping bag. "I feel guilty using an air mattress to sleep on, but age has its privileges!"

"The first one awake starts the fireplace for hot tea." Carl affectionately squeezed his father's shoulder.

The evening was like every other night in the deep Maine woods. The only source of light came from the stars, and they never penetrated the heavy canopies. It was impossible to see your hand in front of your face. Carl instantly fell asleep. Jon heard his soft breathing. He had discovered, on this outing, that his son was no longer a little boy, and that made him proud.

The dawn came with a few scattered cumulus clouds around the sun in the East. They had listened to a weather forecast the night before on the truck radio that predicted sunshine with no moisture in sight – a perfect day for hiking. Jon had hiked several of the trails over the years alone and with friends. Jon and Carl had studied maps of the area and decided on a plan that would take them to the peaks and back down to the campground trailhead where they left the truck with their sleeping bags stored in the locked cab. Their route looked like an inverted U. They anxiously ate two eggs, two donuts and several cups of hot tea for energy and stamina.

A half hour after they climbed out of their sleeping bags, they were on the trail leading to a point near the higher elevations known as Pamola, west of the highest point on the mountain. This was the steepest part of the climb that would eventually take them to the Baxter Peak and South Peak. Baxter Peak is the highest point of land in the continental United States where the first rays of sunshine announce a new day is born.

Carl and Jon took several short breathers along the way. The secret for saving energy during a demanding hike is to completely relax whenever a stop takes place. That could be leaning against a tree or sitting so that all limbs are relaxed. The trails at Baxter are never cleared paths like some parks; instead they are left in their natural state with roots and rocks scattered along the way and encroaching vegetation where it has a chance to grow. Very few improvements were made on the trails or any other portions of the Baxter State Park in keeping with the desire of the original owner. Jon liked the concept of "forever wild." Every visitor was admonished to carry out any waste they produced during their stay. There were no refuse containers that needed maintenance. Rarely was the "carry in-carry out" concept violated.

The large granite and slate formations that made up the mountain were dotted with numerous streams and small ponds filled with crystal clear water. Jon told his son that they were going to use the water in their canteens on their belts. "The water in the ponds or streams may be okay, but my advice is to stick with what you know is pure."

69

The brisk winds during the hike to the peak usually kept mosquitoes and black flies at a minimum. That changes when a rest stop is called. Underneath the canopies where there is less wind, they can be a maddening nuisance unless the hiker comes prepared with either a net over his head, or ample supplies of insect repellant.

Carl soon learned that his father was very much at ease in the wilderness environment. His outlook and countenance took on a more positive and relaxed attitude. His ability to overcome challenges came from his experience and training as a soldier and the years he had spent in the forest as a land surveyor. The wilderness seems to empower man to find strength from within. His father was much more reflective and relaxed in the forest than he was in everyday life. He would look at some distant point with great intensity, blocking out everything around him. It was either a reflection of unspeakable images from the two wars, or it was his father's way of solving problems and issues. It never left him sad or morbid; to the contrary, it empowered him.

Once during the climb when they took a break near the top, a short ways from the junction of two trails called Pamona, Carl asked his father: "Dad, I've been thinking about what you told me about Mom. Was there a part of her Ashley and I never knew that triggered what took place?"

Jon was not surprised that Carl would ask that kind of a question. "You ask the same question that has driven me crazy ever since the accident two years ago. The answer is no, an emphatic no, Son. Don't punish yourself with the question why. I've prayed for a meaningful answer but have found none. The man that was with her was a complete stranger to me. Not once in our marriage did I ever have a reason to distrust your mother. That's the truth, and that's why nothing fits. So abolish that kind of thinking, Carl. I'm getting better as time passes. I'm unhappy that you and Ashley had to be drawn into the mess, but it has removed a stigma I've been uncomfortable with."

"I didn't mean to dredge up hurtful memories, Dad. I was just wondering," Carl said, following his father's gaze to the southwest. "That's Mount Washington in the White Mountains," he claimed, pointing to a prominent peak on the horizon.

"Yes. It's Mt. Washington, Son. I once drove, with your mother a 1936 Ford coupe with mechanical brakes up to the peak. The smooth running V/8 climbed it easily, but the trip down was scary," Jon recalled, laughing about the incident. "That kind of brakes took a good stiff leg to drag the wheels. A lot of the Fords of that vintage had broken seat supports from people pushing the brake pedal with too much pressure. Ford eventually placed hydraulic brakes on their vehicles in 1939.

"I don't see any sign of the Army Air Corps plane that crashed in the northern extremity of Baxter Park. The Air Corps removed most of the important equipment and left the fuselage for such a time as they could lift it out with helicopters. We should be able to see it when we get to the Pamona juncture."

"I thought I was in pretty good shape, but these slopes exercise muscles we don't commonly use," Carl admitted to his father as they started up the trail again.

"I've been thinking the same thing. I attributed it to old age," he chuckled.

They arrived an hour later at the Pamona trail crossing where they were blessed with a magnificent 360 degree view. The sun was out full, and the wind swept across the peaks at a fast pace as Jon and Carl turned to take the trail known as the Knife Edge. It ran southwest to the South Peak, and then tilted northwest to the highest point in the mountain chain, Baxter Peak. The panoramic views were beautiful beyond words to describe them. The arduous climb to the top was rewarded with scenes one can only appreciate after they have made the effort to arrive at such a vantage point.

So far they had not met any other hikers. The Knife Edge Trail was not an easy one. It ran approximately along the higher contour lines to the peaks. There were no improved pathways. The trail followed along the top of a steep ridge with slopes so steep it was impossible to stand or walk. It was like balancing oneself on the ridge of a steep roof, except that there were jagged pieces of slate and granite that could easily trip a hiker and throw him off balance, resulting in severe injury or death. The slopes on either side were several hundred feet long.

Jon suggested to Carl that they eat lunch on Baxter Peak a little over a mile at the end of the trail. "This portion of the trail can be treacherous, Son. If you feel yourself slipping or falling,

71

try to throw yourself across the peak. Some hikers crawl along this peak. We'll be fine if we go easy."

They traveled a few feet apart one step at a time. Jon set the pace. At times the sun was directly in front of their line of travel. Jon had insisted that they bring sunglasses for this portion of the trail. They had progressed for about a half hour when they began to hear desperate shouts ahead of them. They had spotted a group on the trail in the distance and had slowly gained on them. The closer they got, the louder the screams for help became.

"Help… help…someone help us…!"

Chapter Eleven

The screams could not be dismissed. There was an element of fear that alerted Carl and Jon to hasten towards the group that had preceded them. The closer they got the more desperate the pleas became. Jon saw the group of three women on the trail. They were sitting on the peak hanging onto protruding rocks. Another woman was off the trail about twenty feet, clinging desperately to a lone rock outcrop that kept her from plunging farther down the slope. They were all screaming for help.

Jon replied in a loud voice: "We hear you and are coming." He saw no way for Carl or Jon to leave the relative safety of the peak. The slope was too steep to stand on or even kneel. Several minutes later, they arrived at the group huddled in fear. He had seen fear before, but the frightened ladies were paralyzed that they had gotten into a situation that could take the life of one of their group.

The woman hanging on the slope was white with fear and had beads of sweat on her forehead. Blood was oozing from a cut on her left hand. Obviously she was beyond help from any person who tried to reach down to pull her off the slope. Jon grimaced at the situation. Their screaming stopped as soon as Carl and Jon arrived on the scene. The three ladies about Carl's age were too unhinged with fear to be of much help.

"Carl," Jon called, sitting between two of the ladies so that he would be directly in front of the woman on the slope, "remove your packs and have the ladies empty them so that we can use them to extend our reach to the lady in trouble."

Carl knew that when his father spoke in that tone, he was dead serious and expected results. He sat on the edge close to his father and helped them empty the contents of the two packs. Jon turned to the lady beside him and asked, "What's the name of the lady who has fallen off the peak?"

"Her name is Laimi. I'm Carol, and the other two are Jane and Marie who is the last one on the line."

Carol was shaking with fear. They all needed some assurance that Laimi could be plucked from her predicament. If not, death or at the least, severe injuries would be the end result. "I'm Jon, and this is my son, Carl. We need all of you to help us to bring Laimi to safety. Do any of you ladies have a belt?"

Marie was quick to speak up. "Yes, I have one holding my water canteen." She kneeled to balance herself and removed the heavy leather belt with a strong brass buckle, passing it to Jon.

Jon and Carl each had good belts. The three belts fastened together should give him enough length to reach Laimi once he was positioned head down towards her. "Laimi, do you hear me?"

She had been watching what was taking place with alert eyes. She still clutched the sharp protruding rock that had successfully held her in position. "I hear you. I don't know how much longer I can hold onto this rock. My left hand is numb."

"I understand, Laimi. Be patient, and we'll have you back on the trail in no time. Now, we are making up a line with belts and empty packs long enough to reach you. When I throw it to you, wrap the end around your right hand two times. Be careful not to jerk the line. Once you have securely clutched the belt, slowly release your grip on the rock with your left hand. I'll take up the slack and hold you in place as the line stretches. Do you understand?"

"Yes, I understand," she replied in a hoarse voice.

Carl had quickly fashioned the three belts and two packs into a line long enough to reach Laimi as long as Jon was stretched out to his full six feet. At first Jon tried it by leaning over the peak with his shoulders. The line was several feet short. He turned to Carl and the ladies. "Listen carefully. I want all of you to help hold me from sliding down the slope. You can secure Carl so that he can hold me by the tops of my boots. Carl, you jackknife yourself on the peak and let the ladies firmly hold your legs on the opposite slope. That way I can slide down to Laimi and slowly pull her out of danger, okay?"

"We hear you, Dad."

Marie maneuvered beside Carl's legs and held herself in place with her arm draped over the peak. "We'll hold your son, sir, I'm sure of that."

"Laimi," Jon called, anxious to get a line to her, "I'm ready again. Now do as I told you with the belt end." Once she had wrapped the leather end twice around her hand, she gave the line a couple of tugs.

Jon was really worried now. He had the strength to pull her up, but it would place a maximum stress on the makeshift line. The weakest link could spell disaster if it failed. Laimi called out that she was going to release her hold on the rock with her left hand. The second that took place, she slid down the slope two feet, stretching the line to the limit.

"Hold on tight, lady. I'm not going to let you fall. Now I'm going to pull on the line with steady pressure. You can help by digging in your toes on anything that might give you a little leverage to help us pull you to the top.

She looked up at him with sad eyes. She knew then that she was in trouble if the line failed. She embraced the rocky terrain as if she was glued to it and slowly made progress upward. All eyes were on her.

"That's great, Laimi," Jon shouted to encourage her. A heavy wind swept across the slope. It felt good to cool their sweating bodies. He maintained steady pressure on the line so that she would not slide back again. The outing that had been a source of great enthusiasm had suddenly turned into a potential disaster. Every one of them were eagerly helping to accomplish a miracle. The minute they saw Laimi taking her first crawling step upwards, they were relieved and cheered her efforts.

"You can do it," Marie called to her. Slowly Laimi had worked herself up to the point where Jon was able to throw the packs up to the peak where Marie pulled it taught.

"You're doing great, Laimi," Jon told her. "Just a little more, and I'll be able to grasp your hands in mine."

She was getting tired and looked upward to Jon and the others on the peak with weariness in her eyes. Her left hand was bleeding all over her arm. She was reluctant to use it to assist her in the climb, but did so and grimaced. The fear Jon had first witnessed was no longer present. The wind blew several strands of black hair in her eyes, and she shook her head so that she could see clearly.

"Just a couple more steps, and I'll have you in hand, Laimi. You've been a real trooper. Thank God we were close enough to hear your call for help."

She was too weary to speak. Her eyes filled with tears when Jon clasped her two wrists in his strong hands, pulling her up beside him. "Okay gang, pull me over the peak. Laimi is safe."

Carl and the three ladies yanked him up the slope. Carl caught Laimi's arm and sat her beside him on the peak. Laimi wept in her two hands while Carl gently took her bleeding hand and cleaned it with water from his canteen, wiping it dry with a roll of gauze his father always carried in his pack. Then he squeezed antiseptic cream over the cuts and bandaged it tightly. "There, that should hold you until you get down the mountain, Laimi."

"Thank you, Carl," she replied, wiping her face and eyes. She was still shaking from the trauma, and Marie embraced her and held her for a long time in her arms.

"Let it all out, dear lady," Jon said, placing a comforting hand on her shoulder. He then positioned himself so that he was close to the pile of food and supplies that had been emptied out of the packs. "Carl and I were waiting to eat something on Baxter Peak. Do you ladies have any food?" He looked around and did not see their packs.

Marie answered his question, still holding Laimi. "Laimi and I had two packs with our food supply, carrying them up the steepest part of the climb. When we arrived at the Knife Edge Trail we decided to let Jane and Nell carry them for a while and placed them on the peak of the trail. A heavy wind knocked them down the slope. Laimi tried to retrieve one that had lodged on a rock a few feet from the peak. She then lost her grip and slipped to the point where you two came."

Jon better understood their predicament now. "Well, Carl and I have some food we'll be glad to share with you. I think we all need to refuel ourselves." He smiled. "We have several peanut butter and jelly sandwiches and two small bricks of cheddar cheese. I see that all of you are carrying water canteens. Carl can pass out the sandwiches wrapped in waxed paper. I also have a few candy bars in my shirt pocket. They may be mashed a little, but they'll still taste good and give us energy."

They all sat in line on the peak and devoured the food. That made the packs lighter to carry down the mountain. Jon stood up and studied the panorama from every direction. He had learned during their lunch break that they were all students from a normal school in Bangor. Jane, Nell and Marie were all about Carl's age. Laimi was in her forties. She had coal black hair with strands of white around her forehead and ears. It was also apparent that she was the one they all looked to for leadership. All three of the younger students seemed to have a profound respect and affection for her. There was a quiet air of determination about her that was becoming.

Laimi had been quiet during most of the break. She stood up to absorb the view around them and said in a calm voice: "We should get going, girls. Thank you Carl, and Jon, for helping us when we desperately needed help. Your courage and coolness under stress is something we'll never forget. Do you mind if we accompany you along the Knife Edge Trail?"

"We're all heading in the same direction," Jon replied. "It will be a pleasure to accompany you as far as you want. Where did you leave your vehicle?"

"Laimi drove us to a place near the entrance to the park. Once we are at Baxter Peak, we had planned to go down on the Abol Trail to our parking area," Marie explained.

It was essentially the same route Carl and Jon had planned to use, except that they would use an old tote road at the base of the mountain to get back to their campground. Jon checked his watch. It was noontime.

"If you don't mind, we'll be with you to the base. Our truck is a mile or so from your parking area." Jon explained.

"We'd be pleased to give you a ride back to your truck," Laimi offered. "That's the least we can do for you."

Jon nodded his head in approval. "We'd appreciate that, Laimi. Now that we've satisfied our empty stomachs, let's continue our journey. I'll take the point, and Carl can be our rear guard. If you feel more comfortable making a human chain across the Knife Edge, please do so. Whatever makes you more confident in passing. The only other alternative is to turn back, but we can't do that and make it down by nightfall."

They all agreed not to form a human chain. Instead, Marie suggested that they follow a couple of feet behind each other and to go slow and steady. Whenever they came to a more difficult section of trail they could slow down and hold hands to help one another. Jon had checked their footgear and found it appropriate for mountain hiking. They all had soft sole shoes that did not slip easily.

Slowly and methodically they made it to South Peak and then to Baxter Peak where Jon called for a rest. He suggested that they finish eating any sandwiches and cheese left in the pack. The ladies were glad to have a little refreshment. He held the four Payday candy bars he had in his jacket pocket until this moment and passed them out to the future school teachers. He and Carl had eaten plenty to sustain them until they got to the truck.

The trail down the mountain was easier than climbing, but it did put a tremendous strain on the legs and feet which were constantly being pushed into the toe of their shoes. Jon and Carl were surprised at how well the four ladies handled the descent phase of the trip. Marie told them that they had been preparing for this outing for a long time and exercised so that they would be in reasonable physical condition.

All of the hikers were glad to reach the parking lot where Laimi's Ford Ranch Wagon was located. They looked up to the heights they had just conquered and felt a great sense of accomplishment even though their bodies ached all over. Laimi unlocked the wagon and said, "You two guests can ride up front with me. The girls will have plenty of room in the back seat. There's plenty of room for the packs in the back of the wagon."

She turned to Jon. "We're going back to Millinocket. Your campground is on our way home. I can't speak for the rest of you, but every bone in my body cries out for a good hot shower. Just the same, I'm glad we made the trip."

"Old man time is creeping up on me, too," Jon laughed.

"I thought you ladies did very well," Carl said, holding the door open for them to get in the back seat.

A few minutes later, Laimi stopped beside the Studebaker truck. It was already getting dark. "We got down just in time," Laimi remarked, turning to Jon. "I heard you say that you're a surveyor. May I have a business card if you have some with you?"

"Sure, I've got a supply in the truck glove box," Jon replied, getting out of the Ford to unlock the truck. He selected a card and handed it to Laimi who had gotten out of the Ford with the other three ladies. "We live in Wells, which is a long ways from here. It's been nice, ladies. You've been good trail companions. Carl and I wish all of you the best of luck in your school work. Those students who have you for teachers will be fortunate. Have a safe trip home."

All three of the ladies embraced Carl and then Jon. Laimi was last to embrace Carl. "Thank you, young man." She then warmly embraced Jon and said, "How does one say 'thank you' for what you've done for me? May God be with you, Jon Burke. You and your son will always be in my prayers. Thank you." She then kissed him on the cheek and left.

Chapter Twelve

Jon and Carl drove back to Kokadjo where they fixed a meal consisting of B&M Boston baked beans and the remains of a custard pie they had purchased in Greenville a few days ago. They spent the rest of the weekend relaxing, swimming in the pond, and computing the field work that had not been processed. Their parcel of forest land was beginning to look like a puzzle made up of unique and distinct watersheds. They worked hard to lay out the balance of the property to be documented, hoping that they could complete it the coming week when the crew returned.

Jon told Carl that he had a dinner date with Joan Adams and planned to leave for Wells Friday night.

"I'll go back with you, Dad. Hal invited me to go deep sea fishing with him. It's a weekend he was not on call duty," Carl told him. "It's good that you get out to enjoy yourself more, Dad. I like Mrs. Adams. She's a peach. Ben, Jr. and I were friends all through school. He's in the Army now."

"Joan mentioned that to me. He's in Germany. I'm curious, Carl. What did you think of the four ladies we accompanied down the mountain? Three of them were about your age."

"They were great, Dad," Carl enthusiastically replied. "Marie especially impressed me. She seems to be an alert young lady who handled herself very well in a difficult situation. The other two were scared to death and froze. The older lady you pulled off the slope had an air about her that touched me. Marie told me that she had lost her husband in Korea in 1952. She has two sons that had served in the Army. She had been a commercial pilot and wanted to teach, so she's in school to get her certificate."

"That's interesting," Jon replied. "She was a frightened human being, but she showed a lot of grit when the going got tough. I could picture her being a pilot. Her sad eyes have a way of telling the world that she's living with a lot of pain, probably her dead husband."

He admired people who could remain true to the memories of loved ones. It was a character thing with him. He had felt guilty for the past two years that he could not honor memories of Jill the way a husband should. Her conduct had taken that opportunity away from him, and he felt guilty. Now he carried more anger than grief.

Work had given him an opportunity to change his mind and to occupy his thoughts. The project with five men was going very well. He had separated them into two separate crews with Carl leading one in different portions of the forested parcel of land. Carl was excellent with the transit. Friday came quickly. Jon made up the payroll and immediately left Kokadjo with Carl, anxious to see Ashley and Hal, but it was little Nina who held a special place in his heart.

Nina was talking and walking very well for a two-year old. She had captured his heart like little girls have been doing since time began. She called him "Grandpops." Uncle Carl was just plain "Unc". Small of features with dark eyes and blond hair like her mother, she was like a small adult. Ashley usually did her long hair in two braids on each side of her head so that they covered her ears. She called them "horsey tails". Her uncle joked with her that they were pony tails, and she would laugh. She had played an important part in Jon's ability to handle Jill's passing.

Whenever possible, Jon took her in his truck to get an ice cream cone. She would stand on the seat next to him with her left arm around his neck. Sometimes she played with his left ear and laughed that it felt funny. She was a ray of sunshine in a dark period of his life. He always looked forward to taking her home with him when Ashley and Hal wanted to go out together. It was those times when Grandpops could spoil her all he wanted.

Jon and Carl joined Hal and Ashley for a hot meal of macaroni and cheese, green beans, and salad. It was a treat to enjoy a hot meal that someone else had fixed. Ashley was a good cook. As soon as he was stuffed, Jon told Hal and Ashley, "I hate to eat and run, but I'm anxious to check the mail and see what Joan's schedule is for the weekend. Your father is going out on a date," he chuckled to himself.

"I'm glad to hear that, Dad," Ashley said. "I've often heard it said that affairs of the heart are not the sole prerogative of the young. Older people find it just as intense. Say 'hi' to Joan for me. She was great when I had Nina in the York Village Hospital."

"I'll see you later. Enjoy your fishing trip, boys. I'll stop by for you, Carl, when I head back to Kokadjo."

He filled his truck up with gasoline and arrived home to find a large bundle of mail piled up under the door mail slot. He quickly showered and called Joan before touching the mail.

Joan answered the phone. "Hello."

"Hi, Joan. This is Jon. I just dropped off Carl with Hal and Ashley and am free for the rest of the weekend. We put in a good week's work and should be finished with the field work by next week at this time, a month ahead of schedule."

"I'm glad to hear from you, Jon. I just got in from the nursing home. I'm also free until Monday. I've been looking forward to going out with you."

"It's been the same with me, Joan."

"Do you remember several years ago when the war was over, and you came home? Ben didn't make it. I mourned his death more than anyone can imagine, but that was a long time ago, and time marches on. I've been able to place memories of Ben where they belong, Jon, and that's in the past. He would be the first to want my happiness."

Jon remembered his best friend in high school. Kind, caring, and hardworking always came to his mind when he thought of Ben. They were the virtues that defined Ben Adams. "You're right, Joan. I miss him, too. Have you heard from Junior lately?"

"I got a letter yesterday from him. He's in Germany and likes his duty station there. He wrote that the German people were happy to be rid of Hitler and all the hatred and distrust that permeated the country during his reign of terror. They're grateful to be delivered from the years of fear."

"He sounds like his dad. What do you say if I pick you up tomorrow morning to take a ride up to the White Mountains? We could take a breakfast at Howard Johnson at the Portsmouth traffic circle and then head north on Route 16. I'll bring the coupe instead of the truck."

"That sounds like fun, Jon. Thank you for asking. I'll be ready when you get here," she replied.

"Will eight o'clock be too early?"

"Not for me. I'm an early riser."

"I'm looking forward to it, Joan. Until then."

"Goodnight, Jon."

Later, Jon made a small pot of coffee and sat down to go through his mail. Most of it was advertising flyers. He noticed a letter from Amber Hopkins and opened it to read:

Dear Jon Burke,

It was nice to see you again at Fort Drum. I thought you might be interested in knowing that my son, Lieutenant Alfred Hopkins's National Guard Company was sent to the DMZ in Korea. Two days after his arrival he was wounded in an intense exchange of hostile fire between the South Koreans and Americans and the North Korean military. He's in Japan at an Army hospital now. The doctors have informed him that he will recover from the wounds and be sent back to his unit in about a month or so. I was relieved to learn that.

I enjoyed our conversations at Fort Drum. I hope this finds you and yours happy and able to get on with life.

May the day ahead be more fulfilling and rewarding for you than our past experience.

All my best,
Amber Hopkins

At the bottom of the mail bundle was a card with a Bangor Postal stamp. He correctly guessed that it was from the normal school students. On the back of the "thank you" card was a short note:

To Jon and Carl Burke with thanks for averting a tragedy on Mount Katahdin. May God bless you both.

It was nice that we came off the mountain together.
Laimi, Marie, Nell, Jane.

Jon placed the card in a letter tray and leaned back in his
chair. Laimi's note left him with a melancholic feeling. The two
of them had shared a once-in-a-lifetime experience which made
it special. He closed the light and went to bed. Tomorrow
promised to be a fun time with Joan.

He rose early, as was his custom to watch the birth of a new
day. After shaving and showering, he wolfed down a stale
donut from the bread box. The Studebaker coupe was full of gas
and the oil was level as usual. There was a time when he could
not drive the coupe without thinking of Jill and Lauren
Hopkins, but that eventually faded into obscurity. It was a
beautiful vehicle with its three tone blue paint job and shiny
chrome. Carl had kept it waxed and cleaned for the past
months. It had a smooth running 289 V/8 engine that made it
one of the fastest cars on the road.

Jon was all smiles as he pulled into Joan's driveway. She
had stayed in the same house she and Ben had purchased prior
to the war. She had told him months ago that she had paid off
the mortgage. Joan was waiting on the sun porch facing the
roadway. When she saw the coupe, she picked up her purse and
locked the door on the porch. She was wearing a light blue dress
with a dark blue blazer. It was not her way to wear a lot of
makeup to look like a teenager. Her short hair was pulled
behind her ears with two barrettes.

"You're right on time, Jon," she said, embracing him.

"You look lovely, Joan. I saved my appetite for breakfast in
Portsmouth," he laughed.

"So did I. We have a nice sunny day for an outing. I had
forgotten how racy-looking the coupe is."

Jon held the door open for her and closed it after she was
seated. He was happy to have a chance to spend a whole day
with just the two of them. He never thought of her as anyone
except as a dear friend who shared many childhood experiences
together. They were the same age and had gone through grade
school and high school together in the same class.
Consequently, they could recall many special moments.

"It's been a long time since I had someone take me out," she admitted with a soft laugh.

"You've been true to Ben's memory for years, Joan. I admire your faithfulness. However, there comes a time when life goes on, and fighting the battle is not easy."

"I could write a book on that subject. You would not be so proud of me if you knew how often I simply wanted to walk away from it all."

"You wouldn't be human if you didn't have thoughts like that," he replied, squeezing her hand. "It's been ten years since Ben's death. I wonder, hasn't there been someone who was special to you, Joan? If I'm out of line, I apologize and withdraw the question."

She sat quietly for several moments and answered him. "To be honest, Jon, I haven't been attracted to any man except for a doctor at the York Hospital. My first date since Ben's death was with him about three years ago. Several dates followed at two week intervals. I then discovered that he was going through a divorce in Connecticut. I walked away from the relationship. It hurt, but I was thankful that I could fall in love with someone and have feelings for another man. I took the nursing home job in Kennebunkport to make the break complete. Now you know, Jon. I never told my son, so I'd like for you to honor my desire to keep quiet about the subject."

"That's what friends are for, Joan. I hope you're hungry," he smiled.

"As you must know by now, good eating habits do not go hand-in-hand to living alone. It's a nuisance to cook for only one person, and who likes to sit alone in a restaurant?"

"Ya, I understand. That's why I mooch as many meals as I can off Ashley and Hal when I can get away with it and maintain my respectability. Here we are at the Howard Johnson Restaurant at the Portsmouth traffic circle."

They quietly ordered pancakes and sausage with a pot of coffee. It was then that Jon told her about their experience on Mount Katahdin. "I think Carl was attracted to one of the students called Marie. She traveled ahead of Carl on the trail and they talked a lot about school and laughed together."

She looked at Jon. "You asked me about my private life; what about you? You're a nice looking man who wears forty-five years with grace. Is there someone that has given you pause to think of them as special?" She knew that he vigorously guarded his private life. "I know that it has only been two years since Jill's death. Everyone mourns differently. Jill would want you to be happy."

He hesitated and answered her question with another question. "Tell me, Joan. You knew Jill probably better than anyone in town. What do you think she would do in my shoes? Was our marriage as important to her as it was to me?" He knew that the question would give her a better view into his private feelings.

Joan was surprised and took a sip from her coffee cup. "I knew Jill as well as anyone, and I could picture her having a hard time living alone. She was my best friend, Jon. I cannot and will not speak unkindly of her. These past two years you've withdrawn from our social circle of friends, and I've seen you bitter instead of sad. There's a difference, and I can't understand why. I tell you this because we've been friends for a long time."

Jon had to be careful. Joan was a very perceptive person. Did she know the truth, or had she simply picked up on the intense struggle he's had with Jill's treachery the past two years? "Neither can I, Joan. Let's not spoil our day by discussing past events beyond our ability to control. Let me say that Jill's sudden death in New York has not been easy to accept. You needed space to handle Ben's death; well, I'm going to need time to get my life back together again. I'm trying, Joan; I'm trying. Our date today is an affirmation of the progress that I'm making. Does that make any sense?"

"More than you know, dear friend. I apologize if my curiosity got the best of me. Time is the only healer of such deeply carved wounds. I've been there, and I do understand, Jon," she said, changing the subject. "I haven't been to the White Mountains since Ben was a young man in the Boy Scouts. I was a den mother and agreed to climb Mount Chocorua with them."

"I remember; Carl went with you. It was rough, wasn't it?" he laughed.

"My Lord, I was never so worn out in my life. The boys had to practically carry me down the mountain. It was beautiful up there though. The view was worth all of the sore muscles."

Jon nodded in agreement. "Now that we've finished breakfast, let's head for the hills. We can climb Mount

Washington with the Studebaker coupe. I recently had brake shoes replaced on the front and rear wheels. The Stude automatic transmission will hold the car for the trip down the mountain."

"That sounds like fun, Jon. I'm so glad you asked me out," Joan said as he pulled off the traffic circle onto Route 16 leading north.

They spent several hours slowly driving through Crawford Notch to the road leading to the summit. They stopped to watch the coal driven cog railroad vehicle climb the steep trail to the top. They then climbed the summit road to the peak. They had a clear day with excellent visibility to enjoy the panorama that greeted them from every direction. They took time to eat a light lunch at the summit restaurant.

They laughed a lot about some of their grade school times and the months when they were old enough to take jobs at the Wells Casino area and at Ogunquit for the summer. They were days that were etched on their memories forever. It was a period in their lives when time stood still, and the future was theirs for the asking. Echoes from the past are a treasured part of every person's Memory Lane. Adults often go there to gain strength for difficult times. It was that aspect of Joan's and Jon's childhood experience that they shared together. It was something very special for both of them.

On the way back home, Joan had fallen asleep with her head laid against his shoulder. He could smell the unique Heliotrope fragrance she had always used. She had several of the blood-red plants in her living room. The minute a person walked through the door the subtle aroma greeted them.

She slept until he came to a stop to pay a toll fee over the bridge between Portsmouth and Kittery. "My Lord," she exclaimed, looking at where they were. "I wasn't much company, was I, Jon?"

"I thought it was nice to have you rest your head on my shoulder. To fall asleep while a person is driving is a compliment to the driver. It shows that you trust me."

She was pleased with his response. "It's been a lovely day, Jon. Thanks for asking me to share it with you. I've enjoyed it very much."

Twenty minutes later, he drove into her driveway and stopped beside her automobile. He left the headlights on so that they could find their way to her front entrance on the porch.

Joan unlocked the door and turned to him. "Today has recycled some old feelings, Jon," she said, kissing him with soft lips.

It seemed so natural to hold her in his arms. He knew that she had deep feelings for him and said, "Joan, it's been a long time..."

She placed a finger to his lips and said: "Please don't say anymore. I want to remember this day. Good night, dear friend."

"Good night, Joan," he said, closing the door behind him.

Chapter Thirteen

The summer of 1957 passed into history, leaving memories of moonlit nights and star-studded skies. Jon, Carl and the crew of engineering students completed the project on the Great Northern Paper Company lands in northern Maine ahead of schedule. Jon and his son were glad to be back home. They had a few days before Labor Day when the tourist crowds at the seacoast dwindled significantly. Carl used the time to relax and visit with old friends. Jon spent quite a bit of time with Joan going to the movies at the Wells Beach Pavilion before it closed for the summer. They often went out to eat after the show at different restaurants in the area.

Carl was getting ready to return to college. He had told his father that he would not be able to work the next summer because he had to attend a forestry summer camp session in the White Mountains. It was a required course for the bachelor degree in forestry. The day before Jon was preparing to take Carl to Durham, he noticed in the Portsmouth Herald newspaper that an air show was taking place at the Pease Air Base in Portsmouth.

"What do you say if we stop for the show?" Jon asked Carl over supper the night before. "It should be good. The Air Force Thunderbirds will be performing their precision flying skills with the Sabre jet aircraft. After the show, we can drop you off at your dormitory at Durham. It will be lonely here without you, Son."

"That first month at school I was terribly homesick," Carl confided in his father. "I used to call home often. Mom usually answered the phone and made me feel better. I like to remember her the way she was with Ashley and me."

"As well you should, Son. She was your mother, and she did love you both very much. No matter what took place, that love never changed. You've got to believe that." Jon chose his

89

words with care. He wanted to believe that what she had said to Carl was true, but her actions had forever tainted his love and affection for her. The long ordeal of sorting out what was real and what was deception had drained him, and he no longer looked backward. Memories had been tainted, so he resolutely held out for the future.

"Dad, I've been wondering, and so has Ashley. Is the relationship you're having with Mrs. Adams serious?"

"I've known and liked Joan Adams since I was a little boy. We've always had a wonderful friendship. She's fun to be with and I hope that never changes. The answer to your question depends on how you interpret 'serious'. We're the same as we always have been. I need a little more time to sort things out for the future. Does that answer your question?"

"I guess so, Dad. That air show tomorrow sounds like fun. I'm tired. I'll see you in the morning."

They left Wells in time to get to the Pease Air Base by noon. Traditionally, the air shows were very popular and well attended. Carl was driving the coupe and pulled into a parking space on the base close to the reception center. They were right next to a large display of World War Two airplanes that included B-17 Flying Fortresses, B-24 Liberators and P-38, P-47, P-51 fighter planes. The bubble-top Mustang fighter caught Jon's eye and instantly brought back old memories. Carl had often seen that look on his father's face over the years. They were drawn to the planes.

Jon told Carl how planes like the one on display had saved his life and some of his buddies. "Mustangs like this one saved a lot of lives one day in Korea when we were being overrun by the Chinese. We had been fighting overwhelming odds for four days and nights and were out of ammunition, medical supplies, and food. Suddenly two silver Mustangs arrived to give close ground support to us. They cleared the enemy troops closest to us with machine gun and rocket fire giving us a chance to escape across the frozen Chosin ice to United Nation troops on the western side of the Reservoir. It was a powerful show of force when we desperately needed it."

Carl knew that his father was not one to talk about his experiences in combat. He was like most of the veterans. Over the years he had seen that intense stare into empty space that emotionally transported him to some event he kept to himself.

Even though they relived the same horror stories over and over, they never shared it with family or friends. It was a unique trademark of World War Two veterans. Whenever they met other veterans who had similar experiences, they were able to freely discuss the events. Once his father had answered a young boy's curiosity about how it felt to be in combat where it was kill or be killed. His father had looked at him with sad eyes and said: "You're too young to know, Carl. If one hasn't experienced it themselves, they can never know how it really was, and I lack the words to describe it." He never elaborated on that answer to any of his family members.

They climbed into the interior of several of the bombers. Jon told Carl that Joan's husband, Ben, had been a gunner on a B-17 bomber like the one they were in. He was killed over Germany during a bombing mission. "The bomber squadrons lost a larger percentage of men than any other units in the war."

They jumped down from the plane and walked among the display of Army tanks, trucks, and weaponry. The unique vehicle that grasped Jon's attention was a White half-track. It was steered by conventional front wheels and was driven by a pair of steel tracks like a bulldozer. A quad fifty-caliber machine gun turret was mounted in the open body. The four dark barrels pointed into the sky had a sinister look about them. Jon was quiet as he looked at the menacing weapons mounted in a quadrangle configuration. He softly said to himself, "This machine sure brings back memories."

Carl saw how the truck had affected that private part of his father's world. "Wow, that's a rugged looking vehicle."

To Carl's surprise, his father mentioned that "He wouldn't be here if it wasn't for a truck just like this one. His company was making a hasty retreat from the frozen hills of Korea when they were attacked by a large Chinese force that outnumbered them twenty to one. They burned out four sets of barrels on the quad mount keeping the hordes of enemy troops from overwhelming them. They fired the guns constantly for hours in one afternoon, and the enemy kept coming…"

Jon could still feel the sweat that had run down into his eyes even though it was twenty below zero with the wind blowing across the ice. He remembered…he remembered…. A lot of good men were lost in that frozen hell-hole. Sometimes the flashbacks were just as real as the original event.

Carl was worried about his father. That haunting look on his face beside the halftrack was more intense than he had ever seen before, and it disturbed him.

Suddenly, a voice called out: "Hello, Jon Burke."

Carl turned to see Laimi and Marie standing next to them. The familiar voice broke Jon's visit to the past, startling him. For a moment he was confused. Impressions from the past had a way of transporting him to those times he desperately wanted to forget.

Laimi saw the distress on his face. "I didn't mean to startle you, Jon. Are you all right?"

Carl warmly shook hands with Marie and Laimi. "My father was just telling me that a halftrack like this one saved his life in Korea."

Embarrassed to be caught at such a private moment, Jon greeted the two ladies with grace. "What a surprise. It's nice to see both of you again."

Marie looked at the display in the field and said, "Laimi was anxious to come to this show. She was a pilot with the Women's Auxiliary Ferrying Squadron during World War Two. She flew planes like this Mustang from the states to England and to North Africa. We completed our studies for the week and decided to take in this show. It's nice to see familiar faces again."

Carl pointed to the food concession and asked, "What do you say if we grab a hot dog and a Coke?"

"That sounds great to me," Marie replied quickly.

"I'm going to spend some time looking at the planes on display," Laimi told Marie. "You go along with Carl if you want. I'll meet you back here."

"I'll keep you company if you don't mind," Jon suggested, relieved that his awkward moment had passed.

Carl and Marie were both pleased to spend some time with each other. Jon saw the way that Carl looked at Marie and knew that he was interested in the young lady. He smiled and apologized to Laimi. "When you announced yourself, I was wrapped up in some old memories that never go away..."

"You don't have to apologize to me, Jon Burke. I know about that far-away look. I never experienced combat, but I was close to those who were when we delivered the fighter planes to Europe and Africa. I never fired the fighter machine guns in anger, but I would have vigorously defended our formations if attacked by enemy planes."

Jon saw the determined set to her jaw and had no doubt that this lady would give a good account of herself when necessary. "I'm sure you would, lady. Why did you give up flying for a teaching certificate?"

She hesitated to answer him and then said, "I'm not getting any younger, and my pilot license would be harder and harder to maintain. When I was growing up, a high school teacher had earned my respect and affection. Hopefully I can have a few more years in a less stressful line of work. I piloted a commercial aircraft for a shipping concern ever since the war. It was steady and paid well…"

A loudspeaker interrupted her to announce that the show was about to begin with a fly-over of several different aircraft from the New England Air National Guard forces. Later, they anticipated a return engagement from the famous Royal Canadian Air Force Snowbirds, flying pursuit aircraft in which all six planes function as one while making several difficult maneuvers.

Laimi was attracted to the Mustang on display before them and she started towards it. Jon followed her, noticing the wedding ring on her finger, and he asked, "Is your husband here at the show?"

"Oh no," she was quick to reply. "My husband, Oja, was a second generation Finn from Minnesota. He was killed in the second year of the Korean War. He had also served in the Army in World War Two. He was a fighter pilot and was the main reason that I joined the Woman's Air Ferrying Service."

"I'm sorry, I didn't mean to open old wounds. I also served in both wars as a sergeant in the Army. I received a battlefield commission in Korea and am serving in the National Guard as a company commander."

"I recognized you as a combat veteran up on the mountain. Most men who have served share the same blank stare as a signature expression of that generation," Laimi told him.

"You're a perceptive lady."

"I'll ask you the same question. Is your wife, Carl's mother, here at the air show?"

It was an appropriate thing to ask of him. He turned to Laimi and with a serious expression said, "My wife, Jill, was killed in a car accident two years ago."

"I'm sorry I asked," she said, avoiding his penetrating look. "I was not surprised. Lonely people are easy to spot. Marie also thought you were hiding a lot of pain. I apologize. I did not mean to pry."

"Apology accepted," Jon quickly responded. "Marie seems to be a nice young lady. I think my son is attracted to her," he grinned.

Laimi smiled. "Marie was so excited to see you and Carl. She's a lovely young girl and is doing very well in her studies at school. She tutors several students including me when I get impatient with myself. At my age, it's more difficult to adapt to different circumstances." She pointed to the Mustang and exclaimed. "It's a beautiful aircraft."

"I think you're right," Jon replied.

"My personal favorite was the fabulous P-38 Lightning with two engines and two fuselages. It was faster and had a longer range than the Mustang, but they both were a joy to fly."

"You like to fly, don't you, Laimi?" Jon asked, noting her enthusiasm for the planes.

"I fly as often as I can. The aircraft Marie and I came to Portsmouth in is a two-engine Piper that belongs to a Bangor Flying Club. I rented it for the day. It's parked at the northern portion of the airfield."

"You flew in," he exclaimed.

"Sure, what's so unusual about that?"

"Nothing, Laimi. Most people drive, but you fly, I just thought it was great. My respect for pilots and the planes they fly goes back to Korea. Pilots like your husband made it possible for me and a few of my men to escape from being overrun by the Chinese communists..."

Just then, a flight of three Marine Corsairs buzzed the field in a triangle formation. Jon pointed to them as soon as the planes passed the field and said, "Planes like that helped us a lot in Korea, too."

Laimi understood. She recalled that her husband's last letter mentioned that his squadron flew with Marine and Navy Corsairs and with South African Mustangs in a courageous attempt to keep the roadway open for the trapped Army regimental combat team on the eastern side of the Chosin Reservoir. The thought that her husband, Oja, had been one of the pilots moved her with old memories. She had not thought about that event for a long time. Hearing Jon talk about that period made them more real than ever. Memories of happier times overwhelmed her, and a tear rolled down her cheek as she saw the bubble canopy Mustangs on display. It was a poignant moment she could not deny.

The sleek fighter plane had a similar reaction on Jon. Old wounds were reopened, and he could still recall with stark reality the screams from the wounded men who had been assembled on the few vehicles they had left in preparation for a last-ditch, desperate breakout. The scene was still vivid and real to him. The Chinese hit the trucks from all sides, throwing hand grenades into the beds filled with wounded Americans. He had lost most of his command at that juncture next to a bridge. He relived that chaotic scene time and time again.

The courageous pilots overhead did their best to protect them, coming within feet of the trucks with machine gun fire, but it was too late. The image of roaring Mustangs strafing enemy positions was indelibly imprinted on his consciousness. Only ten percent of his command made it across the frozen reservoir to the safety of American lines. Nothing ever eased the pain he carried from the scene.

"Father," said Carl, returning with Marie, munching on a hot dog. "Father…," Carl repeated.

His son's voice broke the ghostly images that continued to torture his father. "Yes, I hear you, Son."

Marie embraced Laimi who was similarly touched by memories the planes generated. It was a poignant moment that neither Jon nor Laimi could control. In time, the memories would fade, but they would never disappear. The memories were too deeply cast for erasure.

"I'm sorry, Marie," she said, wiping her eyes and blowing her nose. "I thought I was over those kind of moments."

"You have nothing to apologize for, Laimi," Marie explained. "We understand. Memories help to define your commitment to the past."

"I could not agree more," Jon added, a little embarrassed that he had allowed himself to be swept away by memories.

"Sometimes those trips down Memory Lane are just as real as when they first took place."

Carl and Marie were just finishing their hot dogs and Cokes. "I'm tempted to get a hot dog. Why is it that they seem to taste better on festive occasions?" Laimi added, turning to Jon. "Are you hungry?"

"Are you inviting me to join you at the concession stand?" he grinned. "Sure. I can always eat a hot dog. My cooking leaves a lot to be desired, and I'm reluctant to add that Carl's culinary instincts are limited."

"Marie and I will be at the visitor's information stand near the public address system," Carl told them.

Jon was happy that his son was relaxed and content with Marie. He had always been a little bit of a loner, like his father, yet he had a large circle of friends. Carl dated some in high school, but nothing developed that interested him. His desire to become a forester was at the head of his priority list. He talked more freely with Marie than with anyone Jon had seen with his son.

Jon and Laimi spent a little time sitting on a picnic table at the hot dog stand watching the fabulous Thunderbirds go through their precision flying maneuvers. One that particularly thrilled Laimi and Jon was when the four planes came into a central point at full speed slightly above the ground and instantly shot straight up into the sky at full power.

Laimi followed their move with a professional's eye. Jon watched her as she was engrossed in the delicate maneuvers of the sleek aircrafts. When the Thunderbirds' portion of the show was over he said, "You love to fly, don't you?"

"Is it that obvious?"

"I think it's great, Laimi," he responded. He not only saw the enthusiasm for the skill of the pilots, he also saw a tint of sadness that seemed to accompany her in everything she did. It was a subtle thing, and he surmised that she was a lonely person, even when she was in the company of friends.

She knew that Jon was studying her and was uncomfortable with his close scrutiny. She avoided his eyes and pointed to a single plane that was going through severe acrobatic movements. "The pilot of that plane is an old friend. We flew fighters into Africa during the war together," she exclaimed.

The small plane did a series of barrel rolls a few feet above the runway in front of the crowd. It was a display of flying excellence, and Jon was impressed and frightened at the risk the pilot was taking. "Wow, that pilot has nerves of steel," he exclaimed, turning to her. "Would you attempt maneuvers like that, Laimi?"

"My friend was a better pilot than I ever was," she admitted with a sigh. She too had been concerned about the risks her friend was taking. "I lacked the daredevil attitude some pilots have, but I always felt comfortable and at ease in the cockpit."

Jon smiled at her. "Is it my imagination, or am I making something out of nothing? My son talked a lot about Marie after we came off the mountain. He's very attentive to her."

"I think they make a wonderful couple," Laimi replied. "Marie is a very special young lady. I admire her. She's a good student and is inclined to be a little bit of a loner. Her friends kid her about not dating more. It's not just shyness; I think she selects her friends with care."

"She has a champion in you, Laimi."

"Much of that is because I'm old enough to be her mother. She lost her mother to leukemia a year ago," Laimi added.

"I'm sorry to hear that. Carl lost his mother two years ago. She was in a car accident. It was not easy."

"Death is never easy to accept, Jon Burke."

"I'm taking Carl back to the university at Durham after the show. Would you and Marie like to join us? I have a feeling Carl would be pleased if you did."

"I'm sure Marie would like that, Jon. Thanks for asking."

"I could bring you back to your plane. Will it be too late to fly to Bangor?"

"No, I fly by instruments night or day, and air traffic from Portsmouth to Bangor is light anyway," she answered.

Chapter Fourteen

The Canadian Snowbirds were the last to go through their precision flying techniques that thrilled the audience. Six planes flying as if they were fastened together gave a stellar performance. Our proud neighbors to the north were an instant success. Just after the Canadian planes made their final stunt, Jon suggested to Carl and Marie that they could all ride to Durham to drop off Carl at his dormitory.

Marie was quick to react. "That'll be fun," she exclaimed, looking at Carl. "That way I will know what your dormitory looks like when you write."

Jon told Carl that he could drive the coupe; he and Laimi would ride in the back seat. "You can drive. Sometimes it's nice to be chauffeured by my son."

Carl opened the passenger door for Jon and Laimi to climb into the backseat and held it open for Marie to sit up front with him. It was a natural move for him as he had watched his father do that for his mother for years. It was a small way to show respect.

Durham was a short drive from Pease Air Base. The University of New Hampshire was a small campus in a small town. Carl drove through the campus to show them the forestry building and the parade ground where the ROTC held their weekly drill. He continued past the forestry building to the new Kingsbury Hall where the engineering students studied. By then it was past four o'clock.

Carl pulled off the street and turned to his father and Laimi. "It's getting late, and hot dogs aren't very filling. What do you say if we go to a popular Italian restaurant on the Dover Road? After that you can drop me off and go back to the airfield."

"Your suggestion sounds great to me. What about you, Marie and Laimi?"

"We didn't anticipate such gracious hospitality," Laimi replied. "It will be nice to have a meal in a good restaurant. The trip back to Bangor for us will only take an hour or so. Thank you for suggesting it."

"It's not every day that my son and I get to share the company of two lovely ladies," Jon turned to Laimi. "Our encounter on the mountain has introduced us to new friends."

Laimi blushed. "You and Carl have helped to make this a most enjoyable day. Thank you for being a friend."

"Whereas I'm the oldest member of this group, I have the privilege of picking up the tab for the meal," Jon chuckled to himself.

Laimi was amused with his newly pronounced role as patriarch of the group. "You may be the elder, but I'm close to your age. You and Carl have made this a special day to remember. Thank you."

The meal progressed at a leisurely pace. They all had spaghetti and a salad. Laimi assured Jon that she was comfortable flying at night with instruments. The plane belonged to a flying club in Bangor, and she had rented it for the day.

After the meal, Carl drove them to Fairchild Hall on the main road through the town and campus. His room was on the ground floor with a window facing the street. He had a trunk full of luggage and boxes. One piece was an orange crate that he used as a night stand beside his cot. Everyone helped to carry the stuff into his room. Laimi embraced him and thanked him for a wonderful day. Jon gave his son a bear hug, and the two left him to be alone with Marie to say good-bye in private.

"He's a fine son, Jon," Laimi said, walking to the coupe.

"I'm proud of him. This summer has been a revelation for me. I discovered that he's capable of taking on responsibilities when necessary. He was always a thoughtful kid growing up. I never had to prompt him to do the chores assigned to him around the house. His sister, Ashley, required a little more prodding," he grinned, holding the door for Laimi to get into the coupe.

Five minutes later, Marie came skipping out of the dormitory with a happy glow about her. She was a little shy confronting Laimi and Jon who had graciously allowed her and Carl to enjoy a private parting.

"Thank you for waiting, Mr. Burke. Carl and I have agreed to write to each other," she told them, taking a seat in the back.

"That's nice, Marie. You'll find Carl to be a young man who does what he says he'll do. I'm glad that you two have become friends."

The short ride back to the airfield took less than a half hour. It was dark enough that Jon had to use lights for the trip. Several small planes were parked on a special section of the field. The plane that Laimi had rented was a two-engine Piper aircraft. Jon walked with them to the plane. Laimi reached into the passenger compartment and picked up a powerful flashlight so that she could make a safety inspection of the craft before taking off.

Marie turned to Jon and said, "This has been a day I'll always remember, Mr. Burke. Thanks for making it possible." She kissed him on the cheek and climbed into the airplane cockpit.

"What does one say that has not already been expressed?" Laimi asked. "It's been nice, Jon. Thank you for being so helpful. Good-bye." She went into his arms, and they briefly kissed. It was a natural response that surprised both of them.

"Is this 'good-bye' or just 'so long', Laimi?"

"It can be whatever we wish, Jon. Let's keep in touch, okay?"

He released her and helped her climb into the cockpit of the plane. "I want to leave you with this thought. If you ever need me for any reason, please call, and I'll be there."

She turned on all of the interior and exterior lights and went through a routine check of the instruments; then she started both engines. "You're a very generous man, Jon. Thanks again for everything."

Jon stepped away from the aircraft as Laimi called the tower and received instructions for takeoff. She waved to him and taxied the craft to the proper runway. She held the plane in place and ran the engines up to full power and then released the brakes. The light craft became airborne within a short distance. She climbed in a steep turn to the north and shortly disappeared into the night. Jon watched the glow of the plane's lights until they disappeared into the night sky.

He walked back to the coupe, and, all of a sudden, he felt alone. The day had been filled with excitement and fun. It was the first time since Jill's accident that he was able to laugh and enjoy himself. The gentle Laimi had left him with feelings that he never thought would be his to experience. It was only two years since his wife had died. How could it be possible that this was happening to him with a total stranger?

He drove back to Route One and headed for Wells. His head was filled with thoughts of earlier days with Jill and had an uncomfortable feeling that he had somehow betrayed what he had always thought they had together. It was a fleeting thought that left him questioning his feelings toward Laimi. He had never been a fickle person, and questioned if he was getting too involved with a stranger.

The day had been important for Carl and Marie. Jon saw the attraction that existed between the two and was pleased. At times he knew that Carl was lonely. Marie displaced that with a contentment he had never seen on his son's face. All in all, it had been a very good day.

An hour later, he turned into his driveway just as he heard the phone ringing inside the house. He rushed to unlock the door and grabbed the phone. "Hello."

"Oh, I'm so glad I caught you at home, Jon," Laimi exclaimed in an excited voice.

"What's wrong, Laimi?"

"We had just left the coastal region when I switched to a full reserve fuel tank on the plane. For some reason the switch malfunctioned, and both engines shut down from lack of fuel. I was northwest of Wells, close to Sanford, when it happened. I made an emergency landing at the Sanford Airstrip on the Sanford plains."

"Thank God you were near a landing strip."

"Sanford was great. They instantly switched on all of their runway lights. I know that I'm a bother at this time of the evening, but could you come to get us and drive us to Bangor? I knew you lived close to Sanford," she asked hesitantly.

Jon was happy to be a help. "I'll be there in half an hour. I'll be glad to take you to Bangor so that you two can make your classes in the morning."

"Oh, Jon, I feel terrible asking this of you after all you've done…"

"Hush, lady. Remember what I told you when we left Portsmouth? I'm glad you thought of me. I'm relieved that you found a safe place to land in the dark."

"Thanks, Jon."

Jon had just started the coupe when Joan pulled into the driveway behind him. "Hi, Joan. I was just going to Sanford to help a friend."

"It's nice to see you again. I stopped by earlier, but you were not at home. I've accumulated some time off, and for the next few days I'll be free. I thought we might get together. Have you got Carl settled in school again?" she asked.

"Yes, he's glad to be back in school. I may have pushed him too much this summer," Jon laughed. "Listen, Joan, I've promised to take a friend to Bangor tonight. I'll call you after I get back and will tell you about it."

Joan was visibly disappointed and turned to leave. "I'll back out and let you go," she replied.

Twenty minutes later, Jon saw Marie and Laimi standing beside a hangar at the end of the airfield. Sanford was a small community field with limited facilities, but business since the war had been brisk. He saw the Piper in the hangar and pulled beside Laimi and Marie. "Do they know what's wrong?" Jon asked, getting out to open the door for the two ladies. Marie climbed into the back seat and Laimi sat beside Jon.

"It was a close call. The mechanic on duty thinks it's the diverter valve that malfunctioned for some reason. They'll be able to fix it. The mechanics are all certified," Laimi said wistfully, looking at the aircraft in the hangar.

"We should be in Bangor in about three hours. Where do you two stay in Bangor?" Jon asked.

"We share an apartment rented by the school on Essex Street. My home is in Harrison, Maine, on Long Lake. My brother and I live there and share expenses for the family farm," Laimi told him.

"When I was in Korea, I remember that a Major General Frank Lowe came to visit our outfit on the eastern side of the Chosin Reservoir in the mountains of Central Korea. He shared cold C-rations with us for several hours. I think he told me that he was from Harrison, but I could be wrong. A lot took place shortly after he left us. He was acting as the eyes and ears of President Truman, and had a tendency to tell the truth even if it hurt. The men liked his no-nonsense approach to collecting the facts."

"General Lowe was a good friend to my father. His wife was a lovely lady. She was a botanist. They lived at the head of the Lake close to our family farm. My brother and I have constantly been remodeling and repairing it."

"I haven't heard you mention children. Do you have any?" Jon asked, looking in the rear view mirror and saw Marie with her head against the rest, sleeping. "Young people can sleep anywhere," he thought to himself.

"The answer to your question is we did not have any children. My oldest brother was killed in action at Normandy. His wife, my sister-in-law, was caring for their two children when she was diagnosed with leukemia and passed away within two years after her husband's death. I adopted the two children, a niece and a nephew. Alan is a Maine State Trooper stationed at the Wells barracks. Angie, my dear niece, has graduated from nursing school and works in Portland. I'm very proud of both of them. When they became a permanent part of my life, I began living again."

"So Alan's stationed at the Wells facility?"

"Yes, he was going to come to the air show with us but had to back out because he was assigned to the security detail for the President's visit to Maine. He grew up to be a fine young man. He was thirteen when he lost both parents. I did my best to nurture them through their teen years."

"I'm sure you did, Laimi," John said, thinking that there was a lot to this lady sitting beside him. "They were lucky to have you."

"I needed them more than they needed me. Alan was instrumental in suggesting that I give up flying for a less hazardous job. This incident tonight reinforces his reasoning. I was more concerned for Marie than myself, but it could have been worse. God was with us. Sanford averted a potential disaster, and that concerns me."

The thought of a plane crashing into unknown territory in the dark is frightening to anybody. He looked at her. Laimi was crying, holding her head in both hands. He placed a comforting hand on her shoulder. "Go ahead, Laimi, let it out. You seem to always be giving. I'm sure the good Lord was with you tonight. We all have those special guardian angels who look after us.

Your deceased husband is probably one of those angels. I admire your courage and unselfishness and am glad that we're friends enough that you called on me to help when I can."

She remained quiet for several minutes and then leaned her head against the seat. "You've been very kind and generous, Jon. I feel bad that a mechanical problem developed when I had the aircraft. It was my second landing with a mechanical malfunction."

She could still recall the terror of that first incident, and described it to Jon. She was prepared to land a new Mustang she had piloted from the states to a field in North Africa. She was part of a flight of twenty planes all flown by women. She was prepared to land when the tower waved her off because she had only one wheel in locked position. She pulled out of formation and tried to shake the stuck wheel loose. Nothing worked and she was running out of fuel, so the tower directed her to an open field with an unpaved surface, more suitable for a crash landing. She landed below stall speed to minimize the damage to the wing that absorbed most of the impact. It had taken her a while to get over the experience, but she flew another Mustang, ten days later, to the same field in North Africa without incident.

Jon listened to her description of the close calls she had in airplanes and was impressed with the courage and perseverance she had displayed. She mentioned the stories not to brag but to simply describe some of the hazards associated with aviation in general.

Once they passed Portland, Jon took the most direct route to Bangor bypassing the heavier traffic on the coastal route. He was relaxed driving the coupe. It cruised effortlessly at seventy-five to eighty miles per hour. Marie was sound asleep in the back seat. He glanced at Laimi beside him. "The road from here to Bangor is smooth and straight. If you want to lean back and rest, the seat reclines. Just pull the lever to your right beside the seat. I'm going to stop in Augusta for a coffee break. There's a great little diner just off the turnpike that has the best pies in the state, and it's open all night. A lot of truckers use it."

"I am weary, Jon. I'll rest for a while and join you for a cup of coffee. I could drive if you want a break. You can rest. You have a long night ahead of you," she exclaimed, tilting the seat to the rear.

"I'll be okay driving. On my way back, I'll catch a short nap if I need it. Our young passenger in the back seat has already fallen asleep."

An hour later, Jon turned off the highway to the diner. Laimi adjusted the seat to a normal sitting position and said, "A cup of coffee will taste good." She turned to Marie and whispered in a soft voice that they were stopping at a diner, asking her if she wanted to join them. Marie was still half asleep and said she did not want anything and would stay in the car.

The diner had several cars in the parking lot. Jon escorted Laimi into the diner through the front entrance where they were directed to a booth next to a window. "Two cups of coffee please," He ordered. "I'll also have a piece of apple pie with a couple of slices of sharp cheddar cheese."

Laimi told the waitress to double the order and excused herself to go to the restroom.

Just as Laimi walked away from the booth, a woman dressed in a pair of green slacks and a dark green blazer stepped up to the table. "Hello, Jon Burke."

Jon looked up at her and saw Amber Hopkins.

Chapter Fifteen

Jon was shocked to see her. "Hello, Amber," he exclaimed. "I'm on my way to Bangor and stopped for coffee. We meet again un-expectantly." The waitress was serving Laimi and Jon their coffee and pie. "Won't you have a seat?" He asked, making room for her.

"I saw you with a lady," Amber said, taking a seat in the booth opposite Jon.

"Laimi went to the restroom. Ah, here she comes," he exclaimed. Laimi was surprised to see a woman sitting with Jon who introduced them. "Amber Hopkins, this is Laimi Hansen. Laimi, this is Amber Hopkins from Albany, New York."

Amber noted Laimi's inquisitive glance and was quick to reply, "I'm glad to meet you, Laimi. Jon and I had the terrible misfortune to lose our spouses in the same automobile accident two years ago."

"I'm sorry for your loss, Amber. I knew he had lost his wife in an accident." She took a seat beside Amber.

"I don't mean to interrupt your coffee break. My daughter, Eileen, is back in the hotel room in Augusta. She's been helping me collect information from the Maine Historical Society about the Benedict Arnold expedition to Quebec through the Maine wilderness. I've been thinking of making the same trip through the forest before winter sets in. I was going to call to see if you would be available to guide us through the forest to Quebec?"

"I remember you mentioned that possibility the last time we met at Fort Drum. That all depends on your time frame, Amber. I have some commitments for this fall. If we were to do it, sooner would be better than later. Winter comes early in that portion of Maine and Canada," Jon informed her.

"My schedule is flexible," Amber replied quickly. "Eileen is returning to college this week."

Jon studied her with a serious look on his face. "Are you prepared for the hardships associated with such an endeavor?"

Laimi listened to the conversation with interest. "I've flown over that area several times, and it's almost as wild and unpopulated as it was two hundred years ago."

Amber thought about her statement. "I know that it would be a hard and demanding walk. Perhaps it would be better to fly over it and land at some key points of interest along the way. I understand a float plane can operate on some of the water bodies along the route. When I first started this project, I was enthusiastic about pursuing it. I still have that strong desire to work it to a conclusion even though it will be knowingly difficult."

Amber stood up to leave. "I'll give it some more thought and let you know, Jon. It's getting late, and you two have things to do. It was nice visiting with you, Laimi. As soon as I've laid out a workable plan, I'll call you, Jon."

Jon and Laimi shook her hand and watched her leave the diner. Laimi was the first to speak. "Amber's an interesting woman. The accident that took both of your spouses must be a horrible thing to accept. You two have my sympathy. She's a highly motivated woman. The saga of Arnold's unsuccessful attempt to take Quebec is a thrilling story of our young country. It's nice that you two have become friends."

Jon told Laimi about their Fort Drum conversation. "She's been traumatized by what happened." He was unwilling to discuss with Laimi what actually took place. She did not need to know, and he was not willing to inform her. It was a part of his life that he wanted to forget, even though it still haunted him in his dreams. He thought it was strange that he came closer to sharing the truth with Laimi than he did with Joan, a friend since childhood. Joan would have found it hard to accept.

Jon and Laimi finished their coffee and resumed their trip to Bangor. He was quieter for the rest of the trip. Ugly images continued to cloud his reasoning. Amber seemed to fuel those kind of thoughts whenever he saw her. Jon assumed that she, too, had similar feelings, and he was proud of her ability to look positively towards the future.

By the time they passed through Waterville, Laimi had fallen asleep in the reclining seat. Her head had briefly touched his shoulder as he turned out to pass a slower vehicle. A full moon shined brightly in the eastern sky, spreading a warm glow over Laimi. There was something about her that made Jon feel good in her presence. She was forthright, unpretentious, unassuming, and he liked her ability to speak her mind. Life had not been easy for her, and she never complained. Her faithfulness to her dead husband's memory was a virtue he admired above all else.

Jill's death had turned Jon's faithfulness into indifference, even hatred at times. Her betrayal and the magnitude of her deception had left him with a dark legacy he could never share with his friends. That fact troubled him. Amber's presence brought it all back to him. The day that Jill left for New York they had made love, and as he waved good-bye to her, his heart was singing. He remembered thinking as she drove the coupe out of the driveway, how lucky he was to have such a wonderful wife... Every night he laid his head on the pillow, the last thought that ran through his head was the age old question: "Why and when did the deceit first take place?"

Those cruel thoughts returned to him as he was driving. It was a beautiful night, and Laimi's presence beside him was comforting. He wondered if she was capable of doing what Jill had done. He had known her for a very short time, and he found it difficult to imagine her condoning what Jill had so callously planned. Laimi and Joan both had remained true to their betrothed. His experience with Jill was making him suspicious of every woman he met. Would it ever set him free? He was never a jealous person, but now he was uncomfortable with the way he was questioning the faithfulness of women he met. Was it an inherent trait of the female of the species? That question alone made him uncomfortable, and knew it to be false. He knew that several men in his company had been unfaithful to their spouses.

The fact that Jill could violate her vows so easily was a constant fact that made his stomach churn. At times he wondered if he was going mad... Paranoia could make him distrustful of anyone he met, and he prayed for God to help him before it became too strongly ingrained in his consciousness.

Laimi and Marie shared an apartment in a residential section of Bangor on Essex Street. Jon was pleased to note that Laimi had closed her eyes and laid her head against the seat shortly after leaving the diner. It was a beautiful night with a full harvest moon rising out of the eastern horizon. Normally Jon would have been filled with a quiet peace of mind and thanksgiving for the beauty of the night. It triggered memories of when he and Jill shared such simple scenes together. The images were impossible for him to control, and they still hurt.

He was familiar with Bangor and pulled on to Essex Street from the center of town. He was reluctant to wake Laimi to ask her the number of their apartment and stopped beside the road.

Laimi lifted her head as soon as she felt the car stop. "Oh, my, I didn't realize we were already here."

"You've been sleeping ever since we left the diner. What's the number of your place, Laimi?" Jon asked.

"It's 82 Essex Street," she replied, adjusting her seat in an upright position. "I apologize for falling asleep. I really wanted to help with the driving."

"It went quickly for me, Laimi," he replied, turning back onto the street.

"It's that large yellow house on the left." She pointed to a New Englander house with a large porch on the front facing the road. Large maple trees lined the driveway.

Jon did not see the Ford Ranch Wagon in the yard. "Where's your wagon, Laimi?"

She struck her head and exclaimed, "I should have told you. It's at the airport. Oh, I hate being such a bother…"

"Listen, Laimi, I can drop you off at the airport on my way home. It's no bother, really."

"We do need it in the morning," she nervously stated.

Marie was awake in the back seat of the coupe. "Wow, we're here already. You must be tired, Mr. Burke."

"Not as much as you might think, Marie. I'll see you safe inside the apartment and then I'll take Laimi to her car at the airport. I'm glad to have helped. You two were lucky tonight. You could have crashed the plane."

"I'll be back shortly," Laimi said, holding the door open for her to get out of the back seat.

Jon escorted Marie to their apartment, holding a flashlight for her to unlock the door.

"Thanks for everything, Mr. Burke. Carl and I promised to keep in touch," she told him, unlocking the door, then she embraced him. "It's been a swell day even if we did have to make an emergency landing at Sanford."

"Goodnight, Marie," he replied. "You'll find that Carl is a young man who keeps his word."

"I'm sure of that; he's a lot like his Dad," she replied, closing the door.

Laimi gave Jon directions for a shortcut to the airport, and within minutes they were parked beside her Ford ranch wagon.

"Well, here we are," Jon announced, getting out of the coupe to open her door.

She searched for the keys to her car and opened the door, throwing her purse on the front seat. Turning to face Jon she said, "I thank you again for being there for us when in need."

"It has been my pleasure, Laimi. I've enjoyed the day. Good luck with your school work tomorrow. I can sleep late if I need to," he chuckled.

"Good evening, Jon. Have a safe trip back home," she whispered in his ear as she embraced him.

He kissed her lightly on the lips and released her, opening the Ford's door, waiting for her to start the engine. She waved to him as she drove towards the entrance to the airport. He watched her Ford disappear and then headed for Route 95.

There was a full moon visible in the west so bright that he could have driven without lights if he had wanted to do so. The ride back home gave him a chance to think about his schedule for the fall months. Perhaps he could help Amber with her plans to familiarize herself with the terrain Benedict Arnold used on his failed attempt to capture Quebec City. He had a feeling that when he said goodbye to her at the diner she was disappointed with his response to her request for assistance.

He felt bad that he had dampened her enthusiasm for the project. It seemed like a perfect challenge for her to spend energy on at this difficult period in both of their lives. He should have encouraged her more than he did instead of suggesting that she abandon the project. He had seen the same sad eyes she had when they had first met in New York. He made a mental note to get in touch with her as soon as he returned to Wells.

It was past three-thirty in the morning when he turned into his yard and drove the coupe into the garage. The front entrance storm door had a letter tucked into the door jamb. He unlocked the door and turned on the lights. It was a note from Joan:

Dear Jon,

I just received a notice from the Army that Ben has been wounded by a grenade at the Korean DMZ. The North Koreans had attacked the post where he was on guard. A vicious fire-fight erupted. The Army warned me that he may lose his left arm.

Give me a call when you get home, no matter what time it is. I need your advice on something.

I'm scared for Ben. He's all I've got in this world, and I desperately want to be with him if possible.

Joan

Chapter Sixteen

Jon's first thought was to call Joan, but at this late hour he hesitated in case she was sleeping. Then, he changed his mind and ran to the coupe so that he could quietly drive past her home to see if she was waiting up for him. If the house was dark, he'd return in the morning. He slowed as he approached the house with his lights dimmed, checking for any sign of activity. Several lights were on in the kitchen, so he quickly turned into the driveway and shut down the Studebaker. She was at the porch door waiting for him to come in.

"Oh, Jon, I'm so relieved to see you," she cried, rushing into his arms.

"You should be sleeping, Joan," he said, holding her. She was disheveled and going on nerves. "Can you tell me anything more than you wrote in your note? I just got in from Bangor."

She repeated that Ben had been wounded by an enemy grenade and was in a hospital in Japan where she was able to speak to his doctor. "They told me that it was too early to determine if he will retain use of his left arm. I've been worried sick since I learned of the accident."

Jon walked her into the kitchen. "He's in good hands, Joan. If it turns out that he'll lose his arm, they are ready to replace it with an artificial one. That technology has progressed a lot since the Second World War, and he'll be able to get along just fine. It'll be a couple of days anyway before they can know for sure. You should be assured that he's still alive. It could have been worse, even though this wound may end his career in the Army."

Joan sat down at the large oak table in the kitchen, resting her face in her hands. "Thank you for coming, Jon. I guess I had to hear that from you. The officer that called reassured me that Ben has not been horribly disfigured."

"Do you have any sleeping pills in the house? Jon asked.

"I'm not sure they'd work on me," she smiled. "I've drank a whole pot of coffee in the past few hours."

"Promise me that you'll go to bed and try to sleep. You've got to be strong for Ben. I'm exhausted, too, and I need some sleep."

"You do look tired, Jon. I needed to be assured by an old friend," she said, embracing him. "You're very kind and caring. Good night."

"Good night, Joan. I'll say a prayer for Ben, Jr. Do you have to work tomorrow?"

"No, I notified them of Ben's injury and that I'd be off for a while."

"Good," he exclaimed. "Let me know if you hear anything new."

Jon went directly home and crawled into his bed. When the sun spilled into the room and lit up his face on the pillow, he dragged himself out of the bed and slipped into the shower. He had always been an early riser and was anxious to have a breakfast of ham and eggs. He put on a pot of coffee first thing. He thought of the day he had spent with Laimi and pondered if his feelings were a little premature for a person he had only met twice. He soon put those thoughts on hold and thought of young Ben, Jr.

Death and serious injuries had been a constant part of Jon's Army career. Frequently unimaginable wounds were inflicted on men he had become close to, leaving a permanent mark on him that he was never able to disregard. Seeing the way Joan was upset made him want to support her. Those who served in the Armed Forces had earned the nation's respect and admiration. Wounded veterans held a very special place in Jon's heart. The fact that he had known Ben since he was a small child placed his welfare, and that of his mother, at the top of his priority list. Sometimes just the presence of a friend made the load of despair easier to handle. He knew that from experience.

He finished breakfast and called Joan. "Hello, Joan, I hope I didn't call too early."

"No, Jon," she answered. "I've been up for several hours, but I did rest well. Thanks for stopping by last night. I was about to call the hospital in Japan for an update on Ben."

"I think you should," Jon replied. "If you don't mind I'm coming over to mooch a cup of coffee from you. I've got some thoughts about Ben's care that I want to share with you."

"I'll put on a fresh pot. Thanks for being so considerate, Jon."

"I'll be over in about fifteen minutes. Find out all you can about Ben's condition and where he's going to be sent after Japan."

"I'll do that as soon as we hang up."

Jon checked his customer appointments to make sure of the time he had available. He had several survey jobs that required research at the Registry of Deeds in Alfred, but they were not pressing. Right now, his friend Joan had priority, and he was glad to support her. His old friend Ben, Sr., would have done the same thing for him.

When he pulled into Joan's driveway, she was collecting the mail in her mailbox. "You're prompt," she smiled at him. "The coffee pot is on."

Jon parked the car and followed her into the house. She looked drawn, and he knew that she had been crying. "Do you have any more news about Ben?" he asked, taking a seat at the large kitchen table where she had placed coffee cups and a large plate of cinnamon rolls.

She wiped her eyes and blew her nose before answering him. "They did confirm that Ben will lose his arm. He also has several cuts and lesions from the fragments of the grenade that will heal without complications. On the way over here I was hoping that they would transfer him to the Boston Army hospital. It's one of the country's best. I was there for a while after Korea."

"I requested that he be moved to the states," she answered, pouring coffee. "The doctor I talked to was the surgeon who operated on his arm," she sighed, avoiding his perceptive eyes.

"You've got to be strong for Ben. His sacrifice is bad enough, but it could have been much worse, as you well know being a nurse."

"I've prayed for his safety every day. I just wish that I could be there to comfort him and help in his rehabilitation."

"I'm sure you'll do that when they bring him to the states. I can tell you from experience that the wounded soldiers in the Army hospitals take care of each other. No one suffers alone.

The brotherhood just doesn't allow it to happen. I have a suggestion for you. How would you like to go to Alfred with me to check out a few deeds? I'll buy you lunch. I know that you're better at reading the small print on some of the older deeds than I am. My eyesight is not as good as yours. Two heads are better than one. What do you say?"

"It sounds like fun, Jon," she said. "When was the last time you had an eye examination?"

"A couple of years ago. I use prescription glasses to read with. My arms were not long enough to read anything," he laughed good-naturedly.

Jon and Joan spent several hours at the county registry tracing titles to several parcels of land so that he could do an accurate perimeter survey for the new owners. Checking on the authenticity of all previous transactions for the lands in question was a tedious job, but it was necessary to verify the ownership status of the current owner. Older deeds had the property lines described as abutting the land of neighbors. Rarely did they give accurate azimuths or distances to describe them. Having a degree of familiarity with older families helped to document the properties. Most banks required an accuracy of one in ten thousandths of an inch before they would accept a loan.

When Joan and Jon were finished at the registry, they ate lunch at a restaurant in Sanford. Jon suggested that they take in a matinee movie at the local theater after they were finished eating. "It will do you good to relax and enjoy yourself."

"Thanks for the interesting day, Jon. I never realized how much effort went into a legal survey of a piece of property. I haven't been to a matinee movie since we were kids," she told him. "I see that *Dr. Zhivago* is playing. A friend of mine at work was telling us about it. It should be fun, Jon."

After the movie, Jon helped her do some grocery shopping and carried the bags into her house. As soon as she unlocked the front door, the phone rang, and she ran to answer it.

"Hello, yes, I'm Benjamin's mother," she exclaimed in a strained voice.

The voice on the other end told her that Benjamin was on his way to the Naval Hospital at the Portsmouth Naval Yard, and should arrive there in three days. It was the best facility in the region for veterans who had lost limbs. Joan turned to Jon and embraced him, thanking God that her prayers had been answered. She shared the good news with him.

"Ah, things have turned out well for you and Ben. I'll be able to stop by and visit with him, also."

The phone call had raised her spirits. "Thanks for a wonderful day, dear friend."

"You've been a good helper, Joan. I should get home so that I can organize the information we collected. I've enjoyed your company and am so glad the day ended on a happy note. Ben will do well in rehab, you'll see." He embraced Joan and left the house.

Four days later Joan called Jon to tell him that Ben was in Kittery at the hospital. "I'm calling to see if you're free to go."

"I'm sorry, Joan. I've got a full schedule of appointments. Tell Ben that I'll be there as soon as possible. Get the visiting hours for me."

"I understand, Jon," she replied, a little disappointed that she could not share the joy of the day with him.

Jon hung up the telephone. One of the reasons he felt committed was an appointment he had made with Amber Hopkins to meet at the old Fort Western in Augusta on the Kennebec River. It was a popular historical location that had served Benedict Arnold as a staging area prior to his difficult trek north to Canada.

Amber was waiting for him at a small restaurant on the bank of the Kennebec River near the ruins of Fort Western. She had taken a cab from the hotel and dismissed it as Jon had suggested over the phone. She was a little nervous to talk about the project. The last time he saw her at the diner with Laimi he seemed reluctant to get involved. She could understand why he might feel that way and decided that she was not going to ask anything of him. He seemed more willing to discuss it over the phone yesterday when he had called her, and that pleased her.

She was determined to continue researching the project. It was important for her to pursue those avenues that would allow her to bring her hopes and dreams to a positive conclusion. She had already contacted the local airport to set up an appointment for her to view from the air the route up the Kennebec and through to Quebec, Canada. She had planned to spend time in the city visiting the locations where Arnold failed in his attempt to lay siege to the city. The people at the Maine

Historical Society were enthusiastic about her interest in writing about the epic project that helped define the young United States of America, and they offered to help her all they could. Now she was even more determined to continue with the research.

Amber ordered a cup of coffee at the restaurant just as she saw Jon looking for her. She raised her hand to get his attention. He smiled and took a seat opposite her.

"We have a nice day to check out a few of the ruins at Fort Western and Fort Halifax. It's nice to see you again, Amber."

"You had a long way to travel," she replied. "After I made this appointment with you I almost called back to cancel."

"Why, Amber?" he asked.

She took a sip of her coffee, noting his quick response. "Well, I had the feeling that I was taking advantage of your offer to help me on this project. It was easy to assume that my enthusiasm to lift me from the throes of despair was shared by someone who had been traumatized by the same events. It was selfish of me, and I want you to know that I'm not a person who takes advantage of people for my own selfish reasons."

Jon recalled their previous meeting, aware that he had been negative in his response to her. "Amber, I apologize if I gave you that impression. I have been very busy. Work has been a salvation for me, and I think your willingness to take on this project is a wonderful thing. I'm proud of you. It's true we have shared an event that could have emotionally crippled both of us. Yet, you had the courage to rise above the horror. I'm pleased to do what I can to help you in that endeavor. I really mean that, Amber."

She looked into his eyes. "I believe you, Jon. My hatred for your wife has been a major event in my life, and without realizing it, I also harbored ill feelings towards you. Your presence reminded me of what happened, and the hurt continued. I've gotten over that, and I apologize. We're both victims of circumstances beyond our ability to control them, and at some time in our lives, we've got to look forward and stop being victims."

"I've had similar thoughts, Amber. My children know what took place. I was feeling guilty, and when they finally discovered the truth, it was a relief for me."

Amber smiled at him. "The twins figured it out before Alfred did. They deserved the truth even if it hurt. Thanks for sharing that with me, Jon."

"What do you say if we put that episode behind us? We deserve a life free of anguish and pain," Jon added. "The years ahead of us have the potential to be happy ones. It may not be the way we had planned it, but it's what it is, and we're the only ones who can make that happen."

Amber was impressed with Jon's determination and logic. "Are you hungry?"

"Yes, I had a donut and coffee early this morning. I think I'll have a hamburger for lunch," Jon replied.

During lunch, Amber told him about her plans to view the route from the air and her tentative plans to go to Quebec and spend some time in the city. Jon was impressed with her methodical approach to the project, and it gave him a chance to study her without the dark clouds of their shared trauma clouding their thoughts. She was a very determined and resourceful individual, and, for the first time, he saw her as the person she was instead of the wife of Lauren, Jill's lover. Both of them had made important efforts to get their lives in order again.

"Fort Western is close by, as you must know. We could start our day off by visiting it," Jon suggested.

"That sounds like fun, Jon. I haven't been there."

Chapter Seventeen

That same evening, while Jon and Amber were touring areas around Fort Halifax and Fort Western, Hal kissed his wife, Ashley, after they had put Nina to bed. He then left the house to attend a grange meeting in Lebanon where he was invited to discuss current fish and game regulations to the members. He always welcomed opportunities to work with the public. It was an important part of his job, and he thoroughly enjoyed the occasions.

After the meeting, he climbed into his truck and turned the radio to the same channel the state police used. He listened carefully to the chatter pertaining to a bank robbery in Biddeford. The suspects had shot a teller and an office worker in the bank. They had escaped in a blue 1962 Chevrolet coupe. Several police officers reported their locations to the Wells Barracks. Hal recognized Alan Bickford who had just reported that he spotted the vehicle traveling at high speeds on Route 202, heading towards the New Hampshire border at Rochester.

Hal was west of Sanford on Route 202 when the Chevrolet coupe with trooper Bickford in pursuit passed him. Alan recognized Hal's truck and called him on the radio, requesting that he follow the Ford cruiser. Assistance was always welcome, and Hal had often assisted his police brothers.

"Hal, the Chevy has at least three men in it. They will resist arrest and are heavily armed. The New Hampshire police are erecting a barricade at the Rochester border, hoping to stop the vehicle. I'm glad you're available, Hal."

Hal increased the speed of the truck and replied to Alan: "My truck is not as fast as your cruiser, but I'm right behind you, Alan. Be careful, my friend."

On a long straight section of the road, Alan saw that there were no cars ahead on the eastbound lane for as far as he could see. This was his chance to attempt an erratic movement to bring the speeding coupe to a halt. Turning his cruiser to the far left of the coupe, Alan then quickly steered his cruiser into the coupe's rear fender pushing the vehicle out of control before the driver could counter the move. The coupe plunged off the road into an alder swamp where the vehicle came to a sudden stop with rear wheels spinning.

Hal admired the grit that Alan had shown and came to a stop behind the cruiser. He turned his powerful spotlight on the coupe when bullets came in rapid succession. One hit Alan in the shoulder, spinning him around. Hal heard Alan cry out in pain, recognizing that he found himself in a dangerous situation. He could not hear any sirens from the backup he knew was on its way. The next few minutes he was on his own! He was concerned that the men would disperse in the swamp and slip away before help arrived. He grabbed his semi-automatic twelve gauge shotgun and leaped from the truck with a strong flashlight in his hand, anxious to get out of the lighted area near the vehicles.

Once out of the light, he saw three men climb out of the coupe with a satchel, probably containing the money they had stolen. They ran deeper into the alder thickets out of the light from the vehicles. In that moment, Hal turned on his flashlight, catching all three men in its beam.

"You three men raise your hands," he cried aloud. "I've got you covered with a shotgun loaded with buckshot."

One man raised his pistol to aim at the light source when Hal pulled the trigger on the shotgun. He heard a cry of pain just as fire leaped from the muzzle of two pistols. One shot grazed his head above his ear and the second bullet hit him in the stomach. He felt a burning, stinging sensation and pulled the trigger on his shotgun two more times, sending a barrage of lead in the direction of the shooters.

Hal dropped the shotgun and fell to his knees, fighting to keep from passing out. He reached for his flashlight on the ground, turning it on the escaping men. Another shot was fired at him. The shot came close to his hand holding the light. Hal pulled his service revolver and placed six shots towards the shooter he held in his light beam.

Two cruisers from Sanford came to a screeching halt just as Hal passed out and fell with blood filling a puddle in the mud. Two officers leaped out of their cruisers, hollering if anyone was hurt. Alan was lying on the ground beside his cruiser and replied in a weak voice, "Hal has been hit. He fired several times with his shotgun and emptied his service revolver. He's in the swamp."

"Hold on, trooper. We've called for ambulances," an officer announced, kneeling beside Alan.

The two Sanford police officers first checked Alan and then entered the swamp to locate Hal. His flashlight was still on and guided the officers to his side. Within minutes several police cruisers arrived at the scene with the ambulances. Several New Hampshire State Police carried the thieves to ambulances to be taken to Rochester for care. Two of the shooters died from wounds received from Hal's weapons. The third one was injured but was able to walk to the ambulance. They located the satchel of money in the swamp and handed it to the Maine trooper present.

Ashley was immediately alerted by the police that her husband was seriously wounded and was on his way to the Sanford Hospital. She instantly left a message on Jon's answering service what had taken place and that she was going to the hospital as soon as she could locate a sitter for Nina.

Amber and Jon were in Skowhegan eating a light dinner after a tiring day of visiting sites along the Kennebec River. Before they left the restaurant, Jon mentioned that he wanted to check his answering service to see if he had any important messages about a couple of projects he was working on.

"I didn't realize it was so late, Jon," Amber said, looking at her watch. "I see a phone booth near the entrance."

"I'll only be a minute, Amber. By the way, do you have a few dimes? I haven't got any change on me."

"Of course," she smiled. "I always carry a small purse for change. Here, use whatever you need."

"Thanks."

The message Jon received shattered his sense of well-being. "I have some bad news, Mr. Burke. Your son-in-law is in the Sanford Hospital, seriously wounded. There was a shoot-out with bank robbers. Ashley called to tell us that she would not be home. That was a half hour ago."

"My God," Jon exclaimed with a sick feeling in his stomach as he walked to the booth where Amber was waiting.

She saw the strained look in his face and rose to greet him. "What's wrong, Jon?"

"It's my son-in-law. He's been wounded in a shoot-out and is in the Sanford Hospital. I've got to head home, Amber."

"Of course, Jon," she replied, leaving money on the table. "Come along, Jon. You look terrible. Do you want me to drive?"

He was in a state of complete shock, living in his own world, thinking about Hal and his beloved daughter, Ashley. What would the family do if they lost the kind and gentle Hal?

He heard her request and answered in a strained voice, "It may be prudent for you to drive, Amber. I'm so sorry that our day had to end this way. Here are the keys to the coupe."

She held his arm and walked with him to the coupe. "This has been a wonderful day, Jon. Right now your family needs you. It's about seventy-five miles from here to Sanford. If you don't mind, I can go with you to Sanford and catch a bus or train back to Augusta. That way I can help you do some driving. I'm a good driver and am comfortable behind the wheel. I've also studied the road system in southern Maine."

Jon's head was spinning with images of Ashley, Nina, and Hal. They would have trouble facing this crisis alone. "Thanks, Amber. I feel helpless right now and appreciate your offer to drive."

Amber closed his door and walked around the coupe to get into the driver's door. She took a few minutes to study the dashboard and instrument panel; then started the engine. "This has an automatic transmission like my Buick. Try to recline your seat and rest, Jon. If I get tired, I promise to tell you. Sit back and say a prayer for your family. I've found comfort in prayer these past two years. It probably kept me from going crazy. Don't worry. We can go south to Route 95 and take it to Biddeford where we can connect to Route 202 which will take us directly to Sanford."

Jon was reassured that she knew where to go and closed his tired eyes. By the time they reached 95, Jon was resting quietly. She smiled at his ability to do so under crisis. He was a good soldier, and she had thoroughly enjoyed their day together.

Amber's first thought when she sat behind the wheel of the Studebaker coupe was that Jill had driven this same car possibly with Lauren in it. Soon, however, those dark thoughts disappeared from her mind. She was strong enough to put that episode of her life in the past and to build for the future a new life. It was either that or the despair would consume her. She had a feeling that Jon had come to the same conclusion. He deserved better. Now his family was the most important thing in his life. She understood that and felt the same way. She was glad that they had become friends after months of living with ugly memories of deliberate and planned unfaithfulness.

Amber drove the 75 miles down Route 95 to Biddeford where she took 111 to 202 which brought them into Sanford. For an hour and a half she had driven steadily at 55 miles per hour. Jon had slept most of the way. The fact that he was able to sleep, or rest, was a compliment to her driving skills.

"You've made good time, Amber. I can't imagine what's running through Ashley's mind right now. I always worried that something like this would happen with the profession Hal chose. He was a good public servant, liked and respected by all who knew him. I pray that God will answer our prayers," Jon was filled with worry and concern.

"My prayers are with you, too, Jon," she replied, grasping his hand. "We'll be there shortly. I've been following the blue hospital signs ever since we entered Sanford."

Five minutes later, Amber pulled into the hospital parking lot, shut off the Studebaker ignition, and passed the keys to Jon. "Here are your keys. I hope I'm not intruding in your family affairs. I can call a cab and take the next bus back to Augusta."

Jon put the keys in his pocket. He recognized Ashley's Rambler in the parking lot. "You're not an intruder, Amber. Thank you for driving. I was selfish and only thought of myself…"

"Hush, Jon," she interrupted. "Your daughter needs her dad right now. Lead the way; I'll follow you."

Jon found a depressed Ashley in a waiting room with a Maine state trooper sitting beside her trying to console her. Jon rushed to take her in his arms. "How's Hal doing, Honey? I got here as fast as possible. We were in Skowhegan."

When she tried to answer his question Ashley cried even louder. The police officer looked on and told Jon that the surgeon was just in to see them. "Hal is in serious condition. A bullet pierced a portion of his heart, and he's still comatose."

The words from the officer hit Jon like a physical blow. He wept for his family and silently petitioned God to be with Hal at this crucial hour. Hal deserved it, and Ashley and Nina deserved His intervention at this time. Good people should be rewarded when it's desperately needed. That old question of "why" returned to his consciousness with a blaze of glory as Ashley wept in his arms. Her world was collapsing, and he was powerless to console her.

"Who is with Nina, Ashley?" he asked in a shaky voice.

"Our neighbor is with her," she answered between sobs of desperation. "I called your answering service, but I didn't call Carl."

"I have the number to his dormitory in my wallet. I can call him from the hospital." He looked at Amber with a forlorn expression on his face. "Ashley, I want you to meet this lady who came in with me. Her name is Amber Hopkins. She was with me when I called the answering service, and she drove all the way to Sanford. Amber, this is my daughter, Ashley."

It was an awkward moment for both of them. Ashley turned to Amber with tears clouding her vision. Suddenly she recognized the name and knew who she was.

Amber saw and understood her confusion, and embraced Ashley. "My heart goes out to you, Ashley, and my prayers have been with you ever since your father told me what happened. I apologize for being a witness to your pain. I hope I'm not an intruder. Go ahead and cry, young lady." She held Ashley's pulsating body close to her heart as tears rolled down her cheeks.

It was a powerful moment for Ashley who heard the soft words of this gentle lady. She knew that her father was going to see her in Augusta, and thought it was a good sign that the pain the two families lived with for two years was healing. Ashley saw the tears in Amber's eyes and said, "Thank you for coming."

Just then a doctor entered the room to speak to Ashley. He had a dejected look about him. Jon's gut instinct warned him that they were about to hear bad news. Ashley was consumed with grief and despair. "Mrs. Perkins, I bring news that will not be welcome. Your husband just passed away on the operating table. I'm so sorry for you and your family. He was heroic in his fight for life, but the damage to the heart was just beyond our ability to mend..."

Ashley fainted and would have fallen to the floor if Amber had not caught her. Two nurses were waiting outside the door for just such an emergency. They quickly placed her on a portable stretcher. Jon was in shock. All of the blood had drained from his face, and Amber was afraid he was about to pass out, too. The police officer helped Amber place him in a chair and asked, "Are you all right, Sir?"

Jon took a deep breath and answered, "Yes, I'm okay. Ashley needs me."

"She's in an adjoining room, Jon," Amber pointed to the door.

Jon carefully got up from the chair and went to be with Ashley, handing her a handkerchief. "Do you want to spend some quiet time with Hal, Ashley?" She nodded her head to acknowledge him and asked the nurses to transfer her into a wheelchair.

"Oh yes, we can wheel you into the ICU room, Mrs. Perkins," said one of the nurses.

Jon knew that this would be a difficult period for his daughter, but he thought it was best for her to be alone for a while with Hal. "I'll be in the next room, Ashley."

Amber was sitting in a chair, holding her head in her hand. Jon took a seat beside her. A Maine state trooper entered the room with Laimi. She was disheveled and on the verge of tears.

"What are you doing here, Laimi?" Jon got up from his chair to embrace her.

Laimi was surprised to see him. "Oh, Jon, my nephew Alan is seriously wounded. I just got the word from the police station and flew into the Sanford airport."

Chapter Eighteen

Suddenly, the world around Jon was crumbling. Chaos surrounded him. First, Joan's son, Ben, Jr., and Amber's son, Alfred, were both wounded in Korea at the Demilitarized Zone; and now, the tragic shootout had taken the life of his son-in-law, Hal. The room was electrified with emotion, and tears flowed freely.

A nurse saw Laimi enter the waiting room and rushed to her side. "Your nephew is in intensive care."

Laimi recognized Amber and extended a hand to her. "We meet again, Amber."

"Jon and I were in Skowhegan when Jon heard about the tragic shootings. I hope you have better news about your nephew, Trooper Alan Bickford."

"I spoke to a doctor on my way to Sanford. My prayers have been answered. Alan will recover and be back at his post in a couple of months," Laimi replied. "My heart goes out to Jon and his family. God seems to take the best we have. Hal was so young and full of potential."

The nurse announced to Laimi. "Come, Mrs. Hansen, you can see your nephew now." Laimi left the room filled with apprehension.

Jon went into the washroom and splashed cold water on his face. He had failed to contact Carl about the tragedy and planned to do so after he freshened up. He left the washroom checking Carl's dormitory number in a small notepad he always carried with him. Amber was sitting beside him. There was a phone in the dormitory mother's room next to Carl's on the first floor. She answered the phone. "Hello."

"Hello, ma'am, this is Carl Burke's father. Would you please have him come to the phone?"

"Yes, it must be important at this time of the night."

"I have to inform him that his brother–in–law has been killed in the line of duty…"

"My goodness," she sighed. "I'll be just a moment, Mr. Burke."

Amber placed a comforting hand on Jon's shoulder. Shortly Carl was on the line. "Dad, this is Carl. What's wrong?"

"Son, I'm the bearer of bad news. Hal has been shot and passed away on the operating table here in Sanford. We're all at the hospital now. Do you have any friends that could drive you here? If not, I'll come to get you. Your sister needs you now. Her world has collapsed, and she's filled with pain so hurtful that none of us can imagine."

"Dad, I hear you," Carl replied in a strained voice. "I don't know of anyone on campus that has a vehicle right now, Dad…"

"That's okay, Son. I'll come to get you."

The Maine trooper in the room was listening to Jon's conversation with his son and took a seat beside Jon, telling him, "This is a sad night for your family, Sir. The New Hampshire State Police can pick up your son at UNH and bring him here to the hospital. What's your son's dormitory and room number?"

"He's in Fairchild Hall, room 101 on the first floor."

The trooper left the room in a hurry, glad to be able to do something useful for the grieving families. Jon excused himself and went into the washroom to splash cold water over his face. Then he went to see his daughter, hoping that he could do something to ease her pain. He found her embracing Hal's lifeless body, consumed with uncontrollable pain. He was concerned for her. The loss of her beloved Hal left her alone and unable to accept the finality of the tragedy. What was she to do without his gracious kindness? He had surrounded her with his love and gentle ways making her feel special. How could she function with that part of their world missing? The ugly question had no answers.

"Dearest, Ashley," Jon whispered in her ear. "If only I had the power to lift this horrible burden from your heart. Honey, you need to go home and take care of Nina. Hal is in a peaceful place and will be with you always."

"But I want to be with Hal," she screamed incoherently.

Amber was given permission to be with Hal and Ashley. She was touched by the trauma she found. She heard what had passed between them and knew from experience what they were going through. "Dear lady," she said, placing her arms around Ashley, "Your father is right, Ashley. I understand why you want to be with your husband. It's only natural, but perhaps you need your daughter as much as she needs you at this tragic time. If your father agrees, I can drive you home in the coupe. I know that you've just been victimized by the most painful news possible. I sympathize for you, my dear girl...I really do. What do you say? I know that I'm a stranger to you, but I want to help wherever I can."

Jon was relieved that Amber's presence had calmed Ashley. He handed the keys to the car to her and turned to face Ashley. "Amber is right, Honey. I'll be along shortly. One of the policemen will drive me. Your brother will be there soon, too. Are you okay with that?"

Ashley shook her head in approval and grasped Amber's hand as she stepped away from the hospital bed. "Nina does need me..."

Jon quickly added: "I know you must be tired, Amber. Ashley has a nice guest room for you to rest in. Carl and I can bunk on the couch in the living room."

"I'll see how things go, Jon. I can always catch a bus to Augusta, or maybe Laimi can drop me off in her plane when she's ready to leave. Right now your daughter needs our help," Amber explained with a determined set to her jaw.

Jon kissed Ashley on the forehead. "Your priorities are correct, Amber."

Ashley seemed content to be assisted by Amber out to the coupe. The cool air was refreshing after the closed atmosphere of the hospital. Amber opened the passenger door of the coupe and helped Ashley into the seat. "I have twin girls a little younger than you, Ashley. I understand the depth of your grief. You must know who I am by now..."

"Yes, I know who you are. My father told us he was going to be with you today," Ashley replied, wiping her eyes and blowing her nose.

While Amber was busy taking Ashley home, Jon was anxious to check on Alan and Laimi. He saw Laimi sitting in a chair beside Alan's bed. He was still heavily sedated. Jon placed his hands on her shoulder and whispered in her ear: "The doctor told us that Alan was going to be okay."

Laimi smiled at him. "Thank God for that. Your son-in-law was not so lucky. I'm so sorry for your family, Jon. The trooper who drove me from the airport told me how courageously Hal responded to a deadly situation. He probably saved Alan's life."

Jon was still having trouble controlling his emotions and nodded his head. "That's what I've heard…"

Laimi understood how difficult the situation was for him and stood up to embrace him. "What does a friend say at such a time? Words seem so meaningless…"

"A hug helps, Laimi."

Jon stayed at the hospital for a while longer. He was worn out and told Laimi that he was going to stay at Ashley's for the night.

Laimi saw the spent look in his eyes. "Jon, ask one of the officers' to drive you to Wells. I'm going to stay until Alan recovers from the anesthesia. I plan to return to Bangor after I hear from him exactly what happened."

"The last time I spoke to Amber she mentioned that maybe she could hitch a ride with you to Augusta tonight."

"I'd be glad to do that. Augusta is an easy airport to get in and out of. It might be late," Laimi answered him.

Jon checked his watch and said, "On second thought, she's probably exhausted like the rest of us. She can sleep in Ashley's guest room. Maybe that's better for her. In the morning she can catch a train or bus to Augusta."

"Well," Laimi replied, "if I don't see her around at the waiting room, I'll assume she's not coming."

"That sounds like a plan, Laimi. I'll say goodnight for now. Alan will be in my prayers. You have a safe trip home."

She embraced Jon and briefly kissed him. "Until next time, Jon."

"Until next time, Laimi," Jon replied and left the hospital with a Maine state trooper.

He found Ashley sitting at the kitchen table crying uncontrollably with Carl fixing a pot of coffee. Jon took a seat at Ashley's side and tried to console her. Nothing he could say or do made much difference. He felt empty and helpless.

Carl told his father that Amber was taking a shower and was planning to stay overnight. "Mrs. Hopkins is nothing like I imagined her, Dad. She helped me get Nina fed and ready for bed. She's sleeping soundly for now."

"That's a good thing, Carl. Mrs. Hopkins has been most helpful to me today. She drove from Skowhegan to Sanford while I rested and brought Ashley home to get Nina at the neighbor's house," Jon informed Carl. "When that coffee is done I could use a cup."

Carl smiled at his father. "I learned how to make coffee the way you like it at Kokadjo this summer. When it's ready I'll get one for you, Dad."

"Thanks, Son. I see that our house guest is joining us," Jon stood up from the table.

"Hello, Jon," she greeted him and took a seat beside Ashley who was holding her head in her arms on the table crying softly. "I just checked little Nina. She's sleeping soundly. She's such a beautiful child."

"Would you like a cup of coffee, Mrs. Hopkins? It's a fresh pot. Father just sampled it and found it strong enough for his taste."

"That would be nice, Carl. Coffee won't keep me from sleeping tonight. The guest room is charming. It'll be a treat to listen to the waves splashing on the shore."

Ashley lifted her head from the table, wiping her swollen red eyes with a handkerchief. Carl placed an arm around her shoulders and gently asked, "Sis, would you like a cup of hot tea and maybe a piece of toast? You've got to eat something even if you're not hungry.

She squeezed his arm. "Okay, Carl, I'll have a tea and toast as you suggest."

Her response pleased Jon and Amber. It was an exhausted and disheartened group of human beings that sat around the table that evening. They were touched by a tragedy in which each individual was searching for a way of handling the reality imposed upon them. Jon found some relief by helping Ashley. Service and the generous giving of himself was therapeutic for him. He was pleased to witness how Amber also gave of herself to the family. It was an inherent characteristic of Army families.

That next morning, Jon was the first to rise with the sun and put on a large pot of coffee. He was in the bathroom when

Joan quietly entered the house as soon as she saw a light in the kitchen. Tears ran down her cheeks as she rushed to embrace Jon. "I was late coming home last night from the hospital in Kittery when I heard the news. My God, Jon, I can't imagine the pain dear Ashley must be experiencing."

Jon was glad to see his best friend. "I loved Hal as if he was my own, Joan. He was so good to Ashley, and he worshipped little Nina... I feel so helpless. It's difficult for me to understand why God has to take the best of us at such a young age. Would you like a cup of coffee? It's ready now."

"Yes, Jon," she replied in a wavering voice.

"So much has happened that I forgot about Ben, Jr. How's he doing anyway, Joan?"

"He's now at the Portsmouth Naval Hospital in Kittery. He's lost his left arm," Joan told him.

"I'm sorry to hear that. I wonder if he knew Amber Hopkins' son Alfred, who was also injured at the DMZ in Korea," Jon said.

"I'm on my way to see Ben this morning," she explained just as Amber walked into the kitchen.

"I just couldn't resist the aroma of coffee," Amber announced, looking at Joan.

"Good morning, Amber. This is an old friend, Joan Adams. Joan, this is Amber Hopkins," Jon introduced them. "I'll get you a cup of coffee, Amber." Amber and Joan shook hands with each other. "Joan and I were just talking about her son being wounded in Korea."

"I'm sorry to hear that, Mrs. Adams. The last time I talked to Alfred, he mentioned that several other men were also wounded in the same exchange of fire. He mentioned that a Ben Adams was the most seriously wounded."

"I just told Jon that Ben lost his left arm and is now being fitted with a new arm. I'm on my way to see him this morning."

"You have my prayers and sympathy, Mrs. Adams," remarked Amber, turning to Jon. "I just checked on Nina and Ashley. They're both sleeping soundly. My heart goes out to them. What a horrible ordeal they have ahead of them."

Joan finished her coffee and got up to leave. "Well, Jon, you've got your hands full here. I'll tell Ben that you'll see him later. It's been nice visiting with you, Mrs. Hopkins."

"I'll be leaving today for Augusta. Tell your son that we're all rooting for him," Amber said, shaking Joan's hand.

"I'll be glad to," Joan replied. "Good-bye Jon. Give my love to Ashley."

Jon embraced her again. "Thanks, Joan."

Amber and Jon quietly watched Joan leave. Amber spoke first. "This has been a difficult time for you, Jon. I can't help but feel like an intruder in your lives at this terrible time. Will you take me to the nearest bus stop or train station?"

Jon looked into her eyes and said emphatically: "You have not been an intruder, Amber. Instead, you've been a very gracious and helpful friend to all of us. Your gentle compassion has touched Ashley at a time when she desperately needed it. Why don't we call to find out what time the next bus will pass through? That way you won't have to wait for a long time."

"That would be nice, Jon," she agreed. "This has given me a chance to know you and your family a little better. It's nice to see how your children are so close to you. At difficult times like this everyone needs a helping hand. I'm glad that I was available to help where I could."

Jon clasped his hands around hers across the table. "I'll phone to see what the schedule is for the next bus or train. Thank you for the kind words. You were marvelous with Ashley and little Nina. Thank you." With that Jon went to use the phone, returning shortly. "The next bus is due at about nine o'clock this morning. The train will be at the station at ten this morning. You pick which one you want to take, and I'll be glad to drive you."

Carl woke up and came into the kitchen just as his father and Amber were getting ready to leave. Ashley and Nina were still sleeping. "Be quiet, Carl, so that they can rest as long as possible. I'm taking Mrs. Hopkins up to the highway to catch a bus."

Carl had observed how the lady had been with his sister and niece. "We thank your kindness, Mrs. Hopkins. I'm glad that I had a chance to meet you. Ever since the accident that took my mother, I've wondered about you and your family. Father has talked very little about the event. Again, thank you, and have a safe trip, Mrs. Hopkins."

Amber reached out and embraced Carl. "You remind me of my son. It was a pleasure to help when help was needed.

Your sister is lucky to have you and your father to lean on. Good-bye and good luck in school."

Jon was impressed with the ease in which Amber interacted with his family. She exhibited a soft gentleness that was felt by everyone. He escorted her to the coupe and opened the door for her. They drove down Eldridge Road, stopping next to Route One so that they could see the bus.

Amber had been in a reflective mood on the way to the bus stop and said to Jon, "It was nice to be needed for a change. Helping others is a wonderful gift to the soul. I return to Augusta a better person thanks to you and your family."

"You've been great, Amber. I've felt a little guilty taking advantage of your unselfishness."

"Hush, Jon. The tragedy that has struck your family will take a long time to heal. Being of service to others is a rewarding virtue that permeates the Army families. I was thankful to be able to help some. You would have done the same thing," Amber stated firmly.

"Here comes the bus, right on time which is unusual," he smiled, opening the door to get out of the coupe to hail the bus. Amber quickly kissed him on the lips. "Good-bye, Jon. Until next time."

"Good-bye, Amber. Until next time," he replied, releasing her. She took a seat so that he could see her. She waved as the bus pulled away, shifting gears.

Jon watched it and felt alone…

Chapter Nineteen

The time prior to Hal's funeral was the most trying and painful period that Ashley and her family ever had to experience. Hal's death at the hands of a criminal created more trauma than the death of her mother. The day that Jon took Ashley to the funeral home to pick out a casket for Hal was the worst of all. Ashley completely broke down, refusing to accept the fact that he was dead and would never be able to see their daughter, Nina, again. Jon held her in his arms, afraid that she would collapse on the floor, and quickly made the selection for the casket, anxious to get his daughter out of the oppressive showroom.

The Maine Fish and Game Department had assigned an officer to be available to Ashley any time of the day or night. The Department also made arrangements for the funeral at the local church they had regularly attended. Six game wardens with their colorful red jackets carried the casket from the hearse to the burial site. A contingent of state police and game wardens made up the color guard and firing squad of seven men.

On the day of the funeral, Hal's mother helped Carl and Jon get Ashley dressed for the occasion. She wore a black dress and a hat with a veil that covered her face. The local doctor gave her a small dose of Valium, a mild sedative, to help calm her for the ordeal ahead. Jon told the funeral director that she was simply not up to a receiving line of sympathizers. The small church was overflowing with people who wanted to say farewell to the popular warden. Law enforcement officers from all of the New England states attended along with a small detachment of Canadian Mounted Police.

Jon had seen Amber park her Buick in the church parking lot and walked solemnly into the church. It was a thoughtful thing for her to do, and it pleased Jon. Amber sat next to Joan who remembered that it was Amber's son that had also been wounded in Korea at the same time as her Ben.

Ashley sat transfixed as if she was in another world during the services. Twice she almost fainted seeing the cold lifeless expression on Hal's face. She kept thinking that he was not dead and that he was going to get out of the casket and take her home. She could feel his strong arms around her. The reality that he would never be able to hold her again was overwhelming.

The minister, who had been a close friend and classmate to Hal, conducted a short service. The good Reverend had a difficult time controlling his emotions and got through the service with a wavering voice.

Carl and Jon escorted Ashley out of the church into the waiting limousine. Tears ran down her cheeks, and heart-wrenching cries for her Hal pierced her lips.

The brief internment service was accompanied by the seven-gun salute to a fallen comrade. The sad refrain of taps being played by a very young game warden echoed across the field of stones. There was not a dry eye in attendance. Jon felt himself becoming a little disoriented as he struggled to hold Ashley so that she did not fall. Carl placed an arm around his waist to steady him.

"Are you okay, Dad?"

Jon nodded his head. "We should get Ashley to the limousine as quickly as possible, Carl. You can help me," Jon had replied in a weak voice.

Laimi had also attended the funeral with her nephew, Alan, who was able to move about with some assistance while his wound was healing. Alan was waiting at the limousine for Ashley. He met her with tears rolling down his face and warmly embraced her. "Dearest Ashley, I'm so sorry that this tragic episode has taken Hal. He was a dear friend. I owe my life to his courageous stand, disregarding his own safety. What does one say at a time like this?"

Jon opened the door to the limousine. "Why don't you ride with us back to the house, Alan? Ashley is not able to attend the gathering at the church hall."

Alan answered with a strained voice, "Thank you…" and carefully took a seat in the vehicle.

Laimi told Jon that the police had given her and Alan a car and driver for the day. "I'll follow the limousine, Jon."

Ashley turned to view the burial site one last time as the limousine pulled out of the cemetery and turned south toward her home. Ashley, Alan, Carl, and Jon rode the short distance to the coast in silence. Jon was concerned for his daughter. She softly wept all the way home, oblivious to those around her. Jon was relieved to be alone away from the well-intentioned mourners who simply wanted to share the grief they all were burdened with.

The limousine pulled into Hal and Ashley's home and stopped at the front entrance. Jon told the driver that he could leave as soon as they got out of the vehicle. "We won't need your services anymore, we won't be going anywhere. Thanks for helping out at this terrible time in our lives."

"You and your family have my sympathies, sir," the driver replied, shaking his hand.

As soon as the limousine left, Laimi and Joan parked their cars so as to not block the driveway. Joan was the first to run to embrace Ashley as she was being assisted up the stairs to the porch. She knew that words at this time were useless and whispered gently in Ashley's ear: "My dearest girl, my heart goes out to you."

Ashley lifted her head and looked at Joan with tears blurring her vision. "What am I going to do without him??? He was my life, my world..."

Jon put his arm around Joan and Ashley. "Come, Ashley, I see that the neighbors have brought little Nina home. You've got to be strong for her, Honey."

Joan let Carl escort Ashley into the living room where Nina was in a playpen watching the people enter the room.

Laimi felt like an intruder. She was a stranger to Ashley and her friends. She grasped Alan by the arm. "Alan, we should leave this family to grieve alone."

Alan shook his head in agreement and gently said good-bye to Ashley as she sat in a chair holding Nina in her arms. "Dear lady, what can one say at such a terrible time? Please know that you are in my prayers. Your husband gave his life for me and I'll try to be worthy of his sacrifice. May God ease the burden you are carrying. Good-bye."

Ashley murmured goodbye and extended her hand to him and to Laimi. "Thank you for caring."

Laimi and Alan briefly said good-bye to Carl and Joan, and Laimi embraced Jon. "Old friend, I pray also for you and your son, Carl."

"Thanks, Laimi," he replied in a hoarse voice.

With that, Laimi and Alan left the house. Joan turned to Jon. "I'm leaving, too, Jon. Please call on me for anything you or Ashley may need. I know it's a hollow message at this time, but I really mean it."

"I know you do, Joan. I'll be in touch. Thanks."

Carl had gone into the kitchen to make a pot of coffee. He saw how the neighbors had stocked the kitchen table with a large array of food. He knew that both his father and Ashley had a sweet tooth and selected a large cinnamon roll from a plate on the table. A sweet bite with a cup of coffee would give them a little energy and help fill their stomachs so that they could rest easier. It helped him when he could do something. Feeling helpless to ease his sister's pain had burdened him all day. He, too, mourned the loss of one of his best friends. Fun memories of their hunting and fishing trips together came readily to mind all day.

Amber left the cemetery with a lump in her throat. Internment services always touched her, and she had been present for many of them over the years. She wanted to send a warm message of condolence to Jon and his family, but seeing how Ashley was so filled with grief, she decided to leave town. She knew that the family needed to be alone to sort out their path to tomorrow, and that had to be done by those who were suffering the most. No one could do it for them. Amber left town and headed for Albany.

Several weeks after Hal's funeral, Jon received a letter from Amber.

Dear Jon,

A few words tonight to tell you that my prayers are always with you and your lovely family. Ashley has been in my thoughts ever since the tragic death of her heroic husband. I attended the funeral and returned to Albany shortly after. You and your family needed time to mourn your loss. I did not want to intrude on that most precious time in your lives.

I want you to know that I have temporarily postponed my Benedict Arnold project. I do appreciate your kind offer to help me thank you. I was able to watch you and your family handle a heart-wrenching tragedy, and you won my admiration and respect. You and Ashley have been tested in a horrible way, and I pray that God will give you the strength to put your lives in order again. Ashley and Nina touched my heart.

My son, Alfred, has been recuperating at Plattsburgh, New York, Army Base and is capable of moving about with some assistance now. His stomach wounds will heal, and he'll be able stay in the Army. I plan to take him to Portsmouth, New Hampshire, to see your friend's son, Ben. I would like to visit Ashley and Nina if it is convenient for her. I'll call when I arrive at Kittery.

I hope this finds you all well.

Sincerely,

Amber

Jon folded the letter and placed it on his desk. He was getting ready to drive to Ashley's with a pickup load of dry firewood for her stove in the living room. The nights were getting cooler. Soon winter would envelope the land. He was planning to go to Kittery to see how Ben was doing with his artificial arm. He had not seen Joan since the funeral.

Ashley was still having trouble accepting the brutal finality that Hal was gone forever and was never coming home. The simple truth shattered her faith and, at times, her rationality. He had asked Carl to stay with her on weekends when his classes were over. Jon made an effort to be with her as often as his work schedule allowed. He was worried for her. She had lost weight since the funeral and ate sparingly, telling him that she could not eat more. Nerves were controlling her stomach, and she was having trouble finding her way.

More than ever she needed the steadying hand of her mother at her side. It was strange; for the past several days Jon thought about Jill more than ever. People were frequently transported back to older traumatic situations so that they mingled with the present, confusing them. Lately Jon had experienced that.

He backed up the Studebaker truck to Ashley's garage and began to pile the wood against the back wall. She came out to help him. She looked drawn and exhausted.

"Ashley, you've got to take better care of yourself. You've lost some weight. Little Nina still needs you as much as ever, and if you become sick, you won't be able to care for her," Jon reluctantly told her.

"I know, Dad," she said, taking a stick of wood from the truck. "I just can't let go. Mourning counselors say that it is healthy to let go. I don't know how, and I don't want to let go of all the things Hal and I shared. He was my life. We had planned so many things with Nina, and now, he won't be there for her. I had bought a new pair of pants and shirts for him. Now he'll never use them. It's just not fair."

"I know, Ashley, I know. I understand, and I feel so helpless because I don't have anything to offer to help ease your pain except for my love and my prayers." Jon embraced her. "You know, I've been thinking more about your mother lately."

She kissed him on the cheek and released him. "That's strange, Dad. I, too, have been thinking about her more since Hal's death."

"I guess it's the trauma of such a loss that makes us revisit those times." Jon stacked the last few pieces of wood and asked, "Can I bum a cup of coffee from you? Afterwards, I'm going to Kittery to see how Ben is doing."

She smiled at him. "I have a fresh batch of apple turnovers that I made last night. They'll go good with cheese and coffee. Nina has not been sleeping very well lately."

Jon was pleased at her smile. "That's only natural, Honey. Babies feel our stress as much as we do, yet they're helpless to express it. I just received a letter from Mrs. Amber Hopkins. She sends warm regards to you and Nina, and was considering a short visit to see you again. She's coming to Kittery with her son, Alfred, to visit with Ben."

"How did Ben know Mrs. Hopkins?"

"Her son, Alfred, is the executive officer of the company Ben was assigned to in Korea. Both of them were wounded at the same time by a vicious skirmish on the Korean border," her Dad informed her.

"I remember how comforting she was for me the time she stayed overnight. Nina really took to her. It'll be nice to see her again and to thank her for her kindness."

Jon had been aware of how Ashley and Nina had responded to Amber's unselfish ways. He visited with Ashley over coffee and then left for Kittery. He assured Ashley that he was going to stay with her that night and promised to start a fire in the fireplace if she would make a macaroni and cheese supper for him. She had agreed to his request and promised to eat better.

Jon took Route 1 to Kittery and turned into the Naval Yard main gate where he requested a visitor's pass to the hospital. He saw Joan's car in the parking lot and was looking forward to seeing her. He had not seen her since Hal's funeral.

He pulled into a parking space on the waterfront and removed the key from the ignition just as he noticed Joan coming out of the hospital entrance with a man walking her to her car. He opened the door for her, and she fell into his arms and kissed him. Jon felt like an intruder, not knowing if he should announce himself or not.

She saw him and pulled from the man's embrace. "Jon, I didn't expect to see you." She felt awkward. "This is Dr. Matthew Withers, Jon. Matt, this is a dear friend of many years from Wells, Jon Burke."

Dr. Withers spoke first, extending a hand to Jon. "I'm glad to meet you, Jon. Joan has spoken often about you."

Jon accepted his handshake. "Joan and I go back to the first grade." He noticed her nervousness. "How's Ben doing?"

"Joan's son is doing very well," Dr. Withers quickly replied. "He'll soon be discharged from the Army, but he'll be able to function with the new arm we've been diligently working on."

"Yes," Joan explained. "Dr. Withers works at the hospital here. I met him at the York Hospital when I was working there. I had mentioned it to you, Jon."

"Yes, I recall that, Joan," Jon mentioned quickly, a little embarrassed to have discovered what had transpired between them.

Chapter Twenty

Jon was anxious to leave the scene. "Well, I came to see Ben. It was nice meeting you, Dr. Withers. I'll see you around, Joan." He then walked into the hospital where a nurse directed him to a ward with a view of the Piscataqua River. He found Ben sitting up in his bed, intent on trying to pick up small objects with his new artificial arm.

"Hello, Ben," Jon greeted him with a hug.

Ben was happy to see him. "Hi, Mr. Burke. I can't imagine what poor Ashley is going through right now. We were great friends in high school. Hal was one of those strong, silent types that you could always depend on when the going got rough."

Jon shook his head in agreement. "You've read Hal correctly, Ben. Ashley is going through a difficult period. Time will ease the pain some, yet pleasant memories with Hal will last a lifetime, and, hopefully, will overcome the grief that consumes her."

"Mom just left. Dr. Withers said that I could soon come home for brief periods," Ben smiled when he told Jon.

"That's great, Ben. I saw your mother in the parking lot." Jon did not want to share what he saw with Ben. "I just received a letter from Lieutenant Hopkins' mother telling me that they are planning to visit you soon. They live near Albany, New York. I met the Lieutenant and his mother at Fort Drum with the National Guard unit from Sanford."

"That would be great!" Ben exclaimed. "I owe my life to Lieutenant Hopkins! After I got hit by North Korean sniper fire, he ran to pull me from an exposed position and took a full burst from an enemy machine gun. Several Americans were hit that day on the DMZ. Exchanges of gunfire is a daily occurrence between the North and South Koreans. I'll be glad to be free of the tense duty. The Lieutenant is a fine officer who looks after his men."

"I'm not surprised to hear that, Ben," Jon replied. "His grandfather was a general officer in the Army. He's carrying on a fine tradition." They reminisced for an hour or so about growing up in Wells. Ben was getting tired, so Jon told him that he'd be back soon to see him and left the building. He was tempted to ask Ben about his mother and Dr. Withers, but refused to bring Ben into the situation. Their warm embrace and kiss bothered him. Joan had told him about an uncomfortable attachment to a certain doctor at the York Hospital. Evidently it had become more serious!

Just as he was starting the truck, he saw Amber's Buick turn into the parking lot. Her son Alfred was with her. He waited until Amber came around the sedan to help Alfred get out of the car. "Hello, strangers," he greeted them.

Alfred recognized him. "Hello, Captain Burke."

"How nice it is to see you again, Jon. Alfred was determined to see Ben, so here we are," Amber offered Jon her hand.

Jon returned her handshake. "Ben told me what happened at the DMZ, Lieutenant." Alfred had a cast on his right foot and his left arm and seemed to be able to use a walker. His mother helped to steady him once he got out of the Buick.

Alfred was a little unbalanced at first and replied, "I was responsible for him. You know how that is, Sir."

"Yes, I understand. Ben will be pleased to see you. I just came out of the hospital."

"I was hoping to pay Ashley a short visit. How is she doing, Jon? I know it's a stupid question, under the circumstances. I've been thinking about her ever since I attended the funeral," Amber told him.

"I saw your car at the funeral, Amber. My daughter will be glad to see you again. She's still having a hard time accepting the finality of Hal's passing."

"Of course. It's only natural. Alfred and I will be along later this afternoon." Amber saw the dark circles under Jon's eyes and knew that Hal's loss was having a profound affect on him too.

"I'm on my way back to Wells. I've been with her most week days. Carl stays with her on the weekends. Do you need a helping hand with Alfred?"

143

"We'll be fine, Jon," Amber smiled at him. "We've got this down to a science."

"We make it slow but sure, Captain," Alfred added with a reassuring smile. "Mom is a little over-cautious, but I love it."

Jon drove the Studebaker back to Wells via the coastal route through Ogunquit. Joan dominated his thoughts. Was he jealous that she had found someone that made her happy? He wasn't sure of the answer. He found Carl already at Ashley's when he arrived there. The minute he walked into the kitchen Carl looked at him and asked, "What's wrong, Dad? Has anything happened to Ben?"

"No, Carl. I'm just tired, that's all," he explained, taking a seat in the living room where he told them that Amber and her son, Alfred, were planning a short visit.

Ashley listened carefully to what her father was telling them. She had been making a large spaghetti sauce from the last of the tomatoes she had picked in the garden. It was Hal's favorite meal, and she knew that her father enjoyed it, too.

"I can smell your spaghetti sauce, Ashley. I feel guilty mooching so many meals from you. That's what you get from being such a good cook." He smiled at his daughter.

"We can have that for supper when Mrs. Hopkins and her son come. It needs to simmer for a while longer," she explained.

"That sounds good, Honey. I saw her at the funeral. She told me that she did not want to interrupt your day of mourning and left shortly after for Albany."

"The time she stayed overnight with me I found her to be a warm person," Ashley recalled. "When we first lost Mom, I often wondered what kind of person her lover's wife was. Once I met her, she was unlike how I imagined her. It was strange for me at first, but very shortly I was at ease with her, and that surprised me."

Jon listened to his daughter. "I can understand how you felt, Ashley. She's a difficult person to define. For a long time after your mother's death, I was troubled when I was with Amber because it brought up old feelings that were difficult to control. I found myself consciously holding her partially responsible. If she had been able to satisfy her husband, he would not have embarked on an affair with your mother."

"But, Dad, that's very unfair," Ashley exclaimed. "What if she thought the same thing about you and Mom?"

Jon shook his head and looked into Ashley's eyes. "I eventually came to the same conclusion, Ashley. Since then I've found her to be a sincere and caring person. Part of her makeup stems from the fact that she came from a military family where service to others has a strong tradition in this country. I've seen that in many Army families who take their vows for duty, honor, and country seriously. That kind of selflessness soon becomes a way of life. Your husband, Hal, had that same sense of duty, Honey. He was not thinking of himself when he answered Officer Bickford's call for assistance."

Ashley saw the serious look on her father's face and answered in a wavering voice, "Yes, I saw that trait in my Hal. I admired it and feared it at the same time."

Jon got up from his chair and embraced Ashley. "I'm sorry, Honey. I did not mean to bring up hurtful memories. How thankful we are for the time that we had him. True love always hurts when the bond is broken."

Carl had been checking Ashley's car in the driveway when he hollered to Ashley and his father, "We've got company. Mrs. Hopkins and her son just drove into the driveway."

"I'll go out to welcome them," Jon said, heading for the front door. Ashley rushed for the kitchen to check her sauce.

Amber was talking with Carl while Alfred was getting out of the Buick. Jon went to him first. "May I help you, Lieutenant?"

"I'll be okay, Captain," he answered. "I just need a little more time to get around. I'm improving every day."

"That's the spirit, Lieutenant. This young man here is my son, Carl." Jon then turned to Amber. "Ashley has a spaghetti sauce simmering on the stove. I hope you and your son are hungry. She's a good cook and enjoys having company."

"That's thoughtful of her," Amber checked on Alfred to be sure that he was okay. "Well, I'll go help her."

"We'll be in shortly, Amber," Jon replied, checking the tires on Ashley's vehicle. "How's the oil, Carl?"

"I just put in a quart, Dad." Carl offered his hand to Alfred. "I'm glad to meet you, Lieutenant."

"Mother told me that you were in school," Alfred gave Carl a warm handshake.

"I'm taking Army ROTC in college," Carl told him.

145

"That's how I got my commission at Syracuse," Carl replied, bracing himself with his cane. "A friend of mine in school had a Stude coupe like this one. We had a lot of fun in it. It ran like a fine watch."

"We're a Studebaker family as you can see," Jon added. "What do you say if we forget titles for now. I'm only a reserve officer. Alfred, you can call me Mister Burke or Jon. Take your pick."

"Well, Sir," Alfred replied. "If you don't mind, I'll continue to call you Captain Burke. My grandfather would want me to do that. Rank in the military is attained the hard way. You have to earn it."

"I agree with the Lieutenant," Carl quickly added, imagining how he would feel being commissioned in the regular Army. "I hope you're hungry. My sister is a fabulous cook."

"We didn't expect such hospitality," Alfred said, feeling at ease with Carl and Jon.

They checked the fluid levels of the radiator and brakes on Ashley's coupe before they joined the ladies inside, where they found the table all set.

They all enjoyed Ashley's dinner topped off with a warm piece of apple pie with a coffee. It was a simple dessert like the last bars of a symphony, ending in a comforting mood. Amber insisted on helping Ashley to clear the table and wash the dishes.

The fall foliage was at its peak in the northern regions of New England. Amber and Alfred had remarked about it on their way to the Maine coast. Amber suddenly had an idea and turned to Ashley. "The colorful splendor of the foliage is beyond compare. It's as good as I've ever seen it. Sometimes a change of scenery can be good for us. You've made wonderful progress, Ashley. Would you like to take a trip up to the White Mountains with us?"

"You've hit on a great idea, Amber." Jon had been thinking the same thing lately. "What do you think, Ashley?"

"I haven't thought about much more than getting through each day, one at a time."

Amber had been feeding Nina some of her baby food and seemed content. "We have a baby seat in the Buick. Since I mentioned it, I'm prepared to pay for an overnight stay at a hotel, and we can return the next day."

It was a very generous offer, and it surprised Ashley. The days and evenings alone had been difficult for her. She thought about the offer and said, "It would be a welcome change to get out of the house. Your offer is most generous, Amber. I hesitate only because of the expense."

Her partial acceptance pleased Amber. "Paying for the trip is not a burden at all. In the big scheme of life, it's only money, and I can't think of a better way to use it. Alfred and I are going to make it anyway. I promise to help you take care of Nina. I think we've already become friends," Amber smiled.

"You're very generous, Amber. It would be good for you, Ashley," Jon said.

"The offer is extended to you and Carl, too," Amber was quick to add. "There's plenty of room in the Buick. Al likes to be my chauffer, but I have to watch him about speeding."

"Mother," Alfred complained with a smile.

Jon was quiet for a moment and mentioned, "I can't go. I have a full docket for the week. Maybe you can go with them, Carl. The foliage is at its peak, and the White Mountains are just spectacular."

Carl checked a notebook in his shirt pocket. "I don't have any real important classes for the next two days. Maybe I could help Alfred with the driving."

It was beginning to get dark, and Amber checked her wristwatch. "This is wonderful. I'm glad I mentioned it. Al and I have reserved a room at a hotel on the coast in Ogunquit. We'll swing by in the morning to pick you up. We can stay at a hotel in North Conway tomorrow night. I'm so glad you've agreed to come along with us, Ashley. You're a very courageous lady and a wonderful mother. We'll make it a fun excursion and take a lot of pictures. Does Nina ride well?"

"Oh, yes, she loves to go for rides," Ashley replied. Jon noted that her color was better now than it was earlier in the day. That pleased him. Amber was good for her.

The next morning was a crisp fall day without a cloud in the sky. Jon saw the Buick pull into the drive close to the house. Carl and Ashley were ready for the trip. Carl rode up front with Alfred. Ashley and Amber sat in the back with Nina between them. Jon saw that Ashley was anxious to have a break from her daily routines. He waved them off and was about to get into his truck when Joan drove into the driveway.

Joan quickly got out of her car and rushed to Jon. "Good morning, Jon. I can't stay too long, I'm on a morning shift."

"I'm glad you came by, Joan." He told her that Ashley and Mrs. Hopkins had just left for the White Mountains. "I've been thinking about what I saw at the Navy Yard."

"I knew that you were upset when you left."

Jon leaned against the truck door and carefully chose his words. "I've thought a lot about you and our relationship over the years, Joan. I knew that you were looking for a commitment from me that I was unable to give."

"Oh my dear friend, Jon," she cried, embracing him. "I've had a terrible night. I need to explain what has happened to me."

"I think I already know."

"Well, the first visit I had to the Naval Hospital I ran into Dr. Withers. The meeting revived the old feelings I thought I had gotten over. To make a long story short, I've fallen in love with him and he has with me. His divorce is final, and we plan to marry this coming Spring. I hope that my best friend can be happy for me. Am I asking for too much too soon, Jon?"

He saw her eyes brighten when she explained what had happened to her. He held her at arm's length and looked into her eyes. "I have to admit I've been upset by what I saw at Kittery. You, my dear lady, deserve the happiness I see in your eyes. I'm a little jealous that I could not be the one, but I'll get over that. If this doctor is all that you believe him to be, then you both have my blessings, Joan. Go for it, lady, and be happy. You tell him that if there ever comes a time when he's mistreated you, he'll have to answer to me. I'll always be your best friend. I've valued your friendship more than you think."

"I'm sure that is true, Jon. Thank you for being you. Now I have to run. You've made my day complete. Thank you."

"Thanks for dropping by."

Chapter Twenty-One

Two Years Later, September, 1959

Jon sat alone at his kitchen table reviewing the past four years of his life. He had a melancholic feeling that always accompanied the end of summer and the beginning of fall. It had been a challenging four years for him, and it all started with the death of his wife, Jill. That had been the beginning of a roller coaster ride that seemed to never end. Hal's violent death had devastated the serenity of Ashley's life, and left him helpless to ease the pain she still carried after two years.

Carl had recently returned to the University for his last year in college. His friend Joan had married the doctor and moved to Exeter, New Hampshire, giving her family homestead to her son, Ben, after he was discharged from the Army. Jon gave him a job to help with his survey work and found Ben to be a good, dependable addition. Carl helped during the summer months, but Jon needed someone on a steady basis.

Carl and Marie were going steady. Jon had seen their attraction for each other ever since they climbed Mount Katahdin. She had obtained her teaching certificate and was teaching the second grade at Kennebunk Elementary School to be closer to Carl. Marie made Carl smile a lot, and that pleased his father.

The trip that Amber had made two years ago up to the White Mountains to view the foliage with Ashley was the first time she had gotten out since Hal's death. She had bonded with Amber and had returned a more relaxed person. Amber and Ashley talked on the phone frequently after the trip. Later in the winter, Amber had invited Ashley and Nina to her house in Albany where they stayed for a week. Ashley had returned with a newly found interest in early American history. Amber had given her detailed tours of Crown Point, Fort William Henry, Fort Ticonderoga, and Saratoga, all within the Lake Champlain-Hudson River area. Jon was pleased to see how Ashley reacted to Amber's gracious ways. She had become a friend to Ashley when a friend was desperately needed.

Amber never mentioned the Benedict Arnold project to him after Hal's funeral. His annual summer training session with the National Guard took him to New Brunswick where he trained with the Canadian Army. He had enjoyed her company that year they had met at Camp Drum, New York, and was disappointed that she had not taken his offer to help. He did get a nice Christmas card from her that same year. The winter months were long for him. Joan was happy with her new husband in Exeter. He occasionally called to see how she was doing. He missed her, and now with Laimi teaching in Guilford, Maine, he spent most evenings alone or with Ashley and Nina.

When she asked him to babysit Nina while she went shopping, Jon was pleased for the change of scene. Lately, Laimi's step-son, Alan, visited Ashley to see if she needed anything. Jon thought it was good for Ashley to have someone in her life. Alan was two years younger than Ashley but his strong sense of values made him appear older. He was a gentle man with an easy-going demeanor that made him easy to approach. He had the reputation of being a good police officer. Jon liked the way he treated Ashley and Nina with respect and compassion. Good manners and common courtesy were slowly becoming lost by the new generation. Laimi had done a good job raising Alan and his sister, Angie.

Jon was on his third cup of coffee when someone knocked on his door. "Come in, the door is open," he hollered. Alan entered the kitchen. "Hi, Alan, I was just thinking about you."

Alan removed his hat and took a seat at the table opposite Jon. He had a troubled look on his face with dark lines around his eyes.

"My God, Alan. What's wrong?"

"I just came from the Portland Hospital," Alan replied in an unsteady voice. "My Aunt Laimi Hansen has had a stroke. She was taken from the Dover-Foxcroft Hospital by ambulance. I was in the Newport area investigating a robbery when I received an urgent call to escort an ambulance enroute to the

Portland Hospital. They gave it a code one which meant a most crucial situation. I never knew it was her, Jon. I never knew until I checked the admittance ticket to the hospital. My sister, Angie, is a nurse at the facility."

Jon was stunned. He left his seat to comfort Alan, placing his hands on his shoulders. "What does one say at times like this, young man?" he asked in a low voice. "I'm going to drive up to Portland to see her. As you know, we've become good friends. She's a wonderful person. What are your plans for the day, Alan?"

"My troop commander told me to take some time off. I plan to return the cruiser to the Wells barracks and get my Hudson. You can ride up with me if you want."

Jon embraced the young officer. Alan looked terrible. "You've got to be strong for your aunt. Before we leave, how about a cup of coffee first and maybe a piece of toast? Something in your stomach will help. Your aunt is in good hands. I suggest that you ride up with me. I'll follow you to the barracks."

Alan held his head in his two hands with his elbows on the table and cried. "Maybe that's for the best, sir.'

Jon poured him a cup of coffee and placed a warm blueberry muffin on the table in front of him. "If you want to call Ashley, here's the phone," Jon said, putting the phone on the table.

"I'll call her from the hospital, Jon. I'm anxious to see how my aunt is doing," Alan declared, walking out the door to his cruiser.

An hour later, Alan and Jon were at the Portland Hospital, requesting information about Laimi's condition. They were briefed by a nurse. "The doctors have determined that your aunt has had a stroke, meaning that she has either clogged or ruptured arteries to the brain. Either condition starves the brain. That's all I can tell you just now. She'll be moved to the intensive care unit after the surgeons are finished. I can tell you that she is comfortable right now."

Jon and Alan both thanked the nurse and retired to the waiting room. Alan was still in his uniform and was looking for a telephone booth. "This may be as good a time as any to bring Ashley up to date. If she tried to call you she must be worried," Alan exclaimed.

Jon pointed to a phone near the cigarette machine. "Tell her that we'll stay as long as possible so that Laimi knows that we are here for her."

While Alan was on the phone, Angie burst into the waiting room with a distressed look on her face. She was a slender young lady with auburn hair and green eyes. She saw that her brother was busy on the phone and took a seat beside Jon. "I'm Angela Bickford, Alan's sister. You must be Mr. Burke. My aunt has told me about you," she said, holding out her hand to him.

"I'm glad to meet you, Angie. As soon as Alan told me about her condition we came as quickly as possible."

"I've been on another floor of the hospital and was unaware that she came in by ambulance until a friend told me who it was." She began to cry and reached into her pockets for a handkerchief.

Jon took her hand in his. "I understand how difficult this is for you and Alan. Your aunt is a wonderful lady. We've become good friends. I pray that all goes well for her."

Angie looked up at him with red eyes. Angie was consumed with worry. "My aunt told me about you, Mr. Burke. She is a very unselfish lady who selects her friends with care. She has been like a mother to me and Alan. We were pleased to learn that she had a friend like you in her life. She deserves the best. I hope you measure up, Mr. Burke."

He was surprised to learn how Laimi had shared her feelings with Alan and his sister. He knew that his relationship with Laimi was something felt more than expressed. They had started by being friends. There was much to admire about the gentle lady who had a passion for flying. "I'm flattered that she shared her thoughts with you and Alan," Jon said, taking her two hands in his. "She's a remarkable lady. Our relationship has developed enough that I admire and respect her very much. Am I measuring up? I leave that to others to evaluate."

"I didn't mean to evaluate you, Mr. Burke," Angie told him. She saw a doctor enter the room and sprang from her chair. "Is my aunt in the ICU yet?"

Jon saw the sober expression on the doctor's face and knew that they were about to receive bad news... The physician embraced Angie and in a strained voice spoke loud enough that they all heard. "We did everything possible for your aunt. There was always the danger of a second attack. She died moments ago with a massive brain hemorrhage. She's with the angels now. I'm so sorry to be the bearer of such horrific news."

Jon felt his knees weaken as he stood up and braced himself on the chair. Alan collapsed in his chair, burying his head in his hands and wept. The doctor helped Angie to a chair beside Alan. Tears slowly ran down her cheeks. She embraced Alan, wracked with pain. Their lives were shredded by the sudden death of their beloved aunt. The finality of the stroke was more than either of them could handle.

Two nurses came into the room to see if anyone needed help. Words were useless at such a time. Jon had turned white, and one of the nurses assisted him back into his chair. He was numbed to the point where tears ceased to flow. It was difficult to grasp the reality that such a caring person was gone from their midst. He immediately regretted that he had never told her what was in his heart. The picture of her hanging desperately to a rock on Mount Katahdin filled his consciousness. At that time he had seen in her eyes that determined spirit which defined the lady. Every meeting he had with her since that time reinforced that first impression. Now she was gone. Finally, tears filled his eyes, and he wept for the loss of a future that might have been, and he wept for Angie and Alan.

The grief-filled room was closed to the public, leaving them to grieve in private. In between the tears and recollections of special moments, Angie was able to explain to Alan that their aunt had prepaid for her funeral expenses and her burial plot in Harrison, Maine, on Long Pond. Alan told Angie that his Hudson was at the police barracks in Wells. Jon suggested that Angie ride with them to Wells.

Alan seemed relieved to do something. "Come with us while I get my Hudson, Angie. You can stay here with me at my apartment. There's nothing we can do for Aunt Laimi now. They'll be taking her to Harrison for the funeral. I'm sure the hospital does not expect you to work until after the funeral. I don't want to be alone."

"Neither do I, Alan," Angie replied, blowing her nose. "Your apartment will be fine. I have two roommates in mine. I never dreamed we'd have to go through this…"

"I know, Sis… I know…" Alan tried to comfort his sister. He looked at Jon who was also overwhelmed by the suddenness of the tragedy. He released Angie and hugged Alan. "Aunt Laimi was touched by your friendship, Mr. Burke. You may not know, but you helped to pull her out of a long-lasting depression that worried all of us who loved her. We thank you for that."

Jon was humbled by his words. "How helpless such tragedies leave us, Alan. Thank you for the kind words. Your Aunt helped me to come to grips with a very crippling personal situation that has burdened me for a long time. I admired the lady very much and will miss her warm smile and spirited determination. You and your sister have a difficult road ahead of you. Well-intentioned words don't help much, but be assured that your wonderful memories will sustain both of you. Time will ease the pain, and time will help to turn those precious memories into smiles instead of tears. Look upon your Aunt Laimi as always being with you as a guardian angel. You won't be able to see her, but she'll be watching from her new vantage point."

Chapter Twenty-Two

Laimi's funeral in Harrison, Maine, was a heartbreaking ordeal for Jon. Her loss was difficult enough for him to handle, but her death reignited the same feelings and emotions he harbored during the funeral for Jill. Even while he was attending Laimi's funeral he was often troubled by the images of Jill that clouded those of Laimi. He wondered if he was going mad and he handled this devastating phenomenon the way he did every personal problem he shared it with no one.

Carl witnessed what his father was going through and intentionally skipped several days of classes at college so that he could be at his father's side. Carl, Ashley, and Marie had attended the funeral with Jon. The small Methodist Church was overflowing with people.

Alan and Angie had grown up in the small rural community. They sat at the front of the church in front of the casket, receiving the outpouring of support extended to them by friends and neighbors. They were numbed by the emptiness of their world. Their beloved Aunt Laimi had graciously led them through childhood with love and compassion. Now she was gone… Angie was beside herself with grief. Alan stared at the open casket oblivious to those around him. He tried to comfort his sister even though his own grief was bursting for release.

The long procession to the small hillside cemetery north of the village proper stopped at an empty gravesite where Laimi was to be buried. The sad fact that this was her final resting place was a sobering reality check for Alan and Angie. The red and yellow colors of fallen leaves were sprinkled on the empty grave. The minister gave a short eulogy for Laimi and read a final prayer as the casket was slowly lowered into the freshly dug earth. One by one the mourners passed the site, sadly dropping rose petals and the traditional handful of soil over the casket. Ashes to ashes, dust to dust...

Jon followed Ashley, Carl, and Marie, briefly pausing at the grave. He had no more tears to shed. The brutal fact that Laimi was never going to be a part of his life left him weakened and filled with a deep sense of loss that he was unable to control. The contorted look on his face as he stared at the casket frightened Carl and Ashley. They gently escorted him to the Studebaker coupe. Marie opened the passenger door for him. The security and privacy of the vehicle was welcomed by him.

Alan and Angie stopped by the coupe to be sure that Jon was all right. They embraced everybody and thanked them for coming. Alan was also concerned how Ashley was handling the situation. She had attended three funerals in the past two years. He helped her into the coupe and said, "Your support means a lot to me and Angie. Thanks for caring. Now the healing must begin."

Ashley whispered in his ear, "I will pray for you and Angie."

Carl waved to Angie and Alan as he turned the coupe around and headed south. Marie had offered to stay with Ashley for the night. Carl dropped them off first. Jon was deep in thought about Laimi and his life without her, and he was worried about the tight schedule imposed on him at the National Guard. They were ordered to move overland to Fort Drum, New York in two days. There was much to do before that could be efficiently accomplished. Some weapons and equipment had to be refurbished, and he was responsible for the estimate of meals, lodging, and medical care of the three platoons under his command. Normally he would have had that accomplished days before the truck convoy left for upper state New York.

Laimi's death was a tragedy for which he would normally have requested sick leave. However, the lieutenant colonel who commanded the battalion became sick from the flu. His absence temporarily placed Jon in charge of the battalion which gave him the added burden of preparing training schedules for two more companies. He was overwhelmed. The day after the funeral he arose earlier than usual, dressed in his fatigues, and was enjoying a cup of coffee when Carl joined him in the kitchen.

"That coffee smells good, Dad. I'll join you. I promised Ashley and Marie that I'd have breakfast with them. May I use the coupe this morning?"

Jon poured his son's coffee. "Sure, I'll take the truck at the armory."

Carl sat at the table and studied his father. There were dark circles under his eyes, and he looked exhausted, yet the day was just beginning. "Dad, are you feeling okay?"

Jon anticipated the question. "To be really honest, Carl, I am weary. This has been a demanding fall so far. With Colonel Peters becoming sick, I've been given more responsibilities. Laimi's funeral was difficult." He did not want to elaborate on the latter.

Carl and Ashley both knew that their father kept a lot to himself. Marie had told him that Laimi and his father were attracted to each other. His degree of remorse at her funeral substantiated that comment; yet, he had never heard his father mention anything about her. "I'm sorry for you, Dad. Laimi Hansen was a very special lady. She had a wide audience that thought the world of her. She was a good person, and her soft presence told the world that she was at peace with herself. She freely gave of herself and will be greatly missed."

"Your description of the lady is accurate, Carl. We became good friends, and I can honestly say that I enjoyed her company very much," Jon confessed to his son, avoiding his knowing glance.

He embraced his son and cleaned his cup at the sink. "I've got a full plate at the armory and had better get at it. Give my love to Ashley and to Marie. When are you going back to school, Carl?"

"Can you take me back tomorrow?" Carl asked, rinsing his cup in sink.

Jon paused a few seconds. "We pull out for Fort Drum day after tomorrow… Why don't you take the coupe to school with you?"

Carl was hoping for that answer. "I'd like that, Dad. I'll take good care of it. I promise."

"Well, the coupe needs a grease job and an oil change. You can have that done while you're at school. Keep your driving to a minimum, understood?" Jon gave him that fatherly stare that he and Ashley had often experienced when he was serious.

"I promise, Dad. I know how much it means to you. Maybe I'll take Marie out to a movie at Kennebunk tonight."

"That sounds like fun," Jon replied. "I like Marie. Is it serious, son?"

"It is, Dad. We have a lot in common, and I like being with her. Ashley thinks we make a cute couple," Carl proudly admitted.

Jon smiled at his son. "I'm glad for both of you. I've got to run. Duty calls."

Two days later, the convoy of National Guard trucks was on the road. Jon was in a brand new-radio equipped Dodge weapons carrier that was to be his command vehicle for the trip and during the ensuing tactical classes ahead of them. He had fallen asleep for a few miles until they reached Albany where they took a half hour break to check vehicles and to enjoy a cup of freshly brewed coffee, thanks to a versatile group of mess attendants who were able to obtain a functioning mobile kitchen on a heavy duty two-ton Studebaker truck.

Several hours later. They pulled to a stop at the famous Fort Drum facility. Jon soon found out that, this year, they were going to be subjected to the most demanding training schedule he had ever witnessed. That night he made his regular rounds to every platoon in his command to make sure that they were well taken care of. He had a great bunch of company commanders, all veterans from Korea, which made his job much easier. That first night, he would normally have gone to the Officers' Club; instead, he went directly to his quarters and went to bed after he called Ashley to inform her that they had arrived on schedule. He was tired and weary and crawled into bed.

The training center made every effort to pack as much training into the two week period as was physically and mentally possible. Jon began to feel relieved after they started their field maneuvers. His newly assigned position as battalion commander actually required less physical effort than his former position commanding a company. He was able to delegate more responsibility.

The second evening, Jon visited the Officers' Club. It was a busy place after hours. He helped himself to a full tray of steak, potatoes and a salad. He turned to locate an empty table and saw Amber waving to him. She was with two ladies and offered to share their table with him.

"Hello, Jon," she said, rising to greet him, motioning for them to take the two empty chairs at the large table. "It's so nice to see you again. My two friends were too lazy to fix supper, so we took advantage of the club tonight. The lady on my left is Colleen Jones, and the lady on my right is Jane Haggerstrom. Both of them are married to retired Army officers."

Jon introduced himself and took a seat. "It's nice to see a familiar face, Amber. After a long day in the field I was starved."

Colleen and Jane had finished their meals and were ready to leave when Amber recognized Jon. They excused themselves and left the club. Jon was concerned for Amber and asked, "Do you have transport to wherever you're staying, Amber?"

"Yes, I have my Buick. Colleen and Jane had arrived much earlier," Amber told him. "Jon, you look tired. Are you feeling okay?"

He knew her well enough to be truthful. "You know, Amber, I've been off lately, and I plan to visit the infirmary tomorrow for a good checkup. I do feel better since we've settled into the training routine."

"I'm so sorry about Laimi's passing," Amber replied, remembering that they had been good friends. "You've certainly had your share of deaths lately. They take a toll on us whether we realize it or not. Ashley has been concerned for you, Jon. We keep in touch quite often. She's a wonderful person. You've done a great job with the two children."

"I think that I've needed them more than they need old Dad," he smiled.

She returned his smile. "You're a good father, Jon. It's not easy to be alone. The time I met you and Laimi at that diner in Maine I knew that you two had a comforting relationship. I was pleased for you. You deserved it… yet, her early passing has had a commensurate amount of pain that's hard to handle."

"You're correct, Amber," he answered in a soft voice. "The loss of such a decent person has been difficult…"

"I didn't mean to bring up hurtful memories, Jon. Forgive me."

Jon changed the subject, feeling uncomfortable. "Is Alfred here at Fort Drum?"

"No, he's in Germany, totally recovered from his wounds." Amber gave a sigh of relief. "I came to the area for a visit to a dear old friend of many years. He's now on oxygen full time and has trouble breathing. He's a retired brigadier general. His son is a retired West Point graduate and has moved in to help take care of his father. We've become good friends."

Jon heard what she was saying but paid little attention to it. He doubled over with an excruciating pain in his stomach, and the room began to turn around him. Amber was quick to kneel beside him on the floor and cried desperately, "Someone help me!"

Soon Jon was lifted from the floor and carried by his fellow officers to a couch in the visiting section of the Club. Someone hollered that they had called for an ambulance. Amber was concerned for him, but she was rational enough to recognize that he may possibly need the services of a full service hospital. The base infirmary was ill-equipped to handle a serious case. The closest hospital was in Watertown, a few miles south of the Fort.

A young captain loosened Jon's necktie and felt for a pulse. "I'm the one who called for an ambulance. They'll take him to the large hospital in Watertown. He's running a fever, and his pulse is racing very fast." He turned to look at Amber. "Are you the captain's wife?"

"No, but I'm a very good friend of the family. Thank you for calling for help. He simply fainted and complained of a terrific pain in his stomach," Amber informed the young captain.

"It's possible that he has burst an appendix or maybe a perforation of the stomach. Either would cause extreme pain. He needs immediate surgical care, and the facility at the Fort is not as well equipped as the one in Watertown," he said.

"You made a wise decision, Captain. Thank you."

"I'm Captain Green. I'm a pediatric doctor here on maneuvers with my regiment from New Jersey. I'm glad to assist, ma'am. The emergency operator told me that they have a standby unit here at the Fort for this type of emergency. I hear it outside now. Don't worry. Your friend will be in good hands."

Room was made for the ambulance attendants to rush to Jon. Within minutes, he was carried out the door on a stretcher to the waiting ambulance. Amber had followed them. Once Jon was pushed into the ambulance, she begged one of the attendants if she could go with them.

"Sure, lady. There's room for you. If the patient wakes up, your presence may comfort him."

She took a seat at Jon's side and fastened the safety belt the attendant held for her.

Chapter Twenty-Three

Jon was immediately taken from the Officers' Club to the emergency room with surgeons standing by. He was in pain and folded himself in a fetal position which gave him some relief. He knew that Amber was with him and reached for her hand. A technician placed a valium tablet in his mouth. Soon it was helping him to breath, and at the same time it made him less aware of his surroundings.

The technician whispered in his ear that they were backing into the emergency room entrance, and within minutes he would be in the operating room. He nodded his head that he understood and looked up at Amber. She released his hand and whispered that she would stay with him and notify Ashley and Carl as they rolled him out the door of the ambulance.

Amber had a worried look on her face. A nurse pointed to a waiting room. She took a seat and dug into her purse to locate a small notebook with telephone numbers listed. Her first call was to Ashley in Wells.

"Ashley, this is Amber Hopkins. I'm at the hospital in Watertown, New York. Your father is in the operating room now. He passed out at the Officers' Club. Would you please call Carl to notify him about your father?"

Ashley was not surprised. "Dad did not look good for several days before he left with the battalion. I'm thankful that you're with him, Amber."

"I'll tell the doctor that as soon as I see him," Amber replied. "I plan to stay with him until he's moved into intensive care. As soon as I have any more information, I'll call you."

"Dad's a strong man who keeps a lot to himself," Ashley explained. "He really hasn't been himself since Mom had the accident. He's been a wonderful father to Carl and me. He has always placed the welfare of the family above his own well-being. He truly deserves some peace and happiness in his remaining years."

"It's wonderful that you think of him that way, Ashley. Probably I'm the only one who can truly appreciate all the pain that accident generated. I knew that your father was going through the same turmoil, especially when we met. I reminded him of what he had lost, and it was the same with me."

"Thank you for telling me that, Amber. Both of you have travelled a difficult road," Ashley replied, pausing for a moment, hoping that the question she was about to ask Amber was not out of line. "Amber," she announced in a trembling voice, well aware that her father would not approve.

"What is it, Ashley?"

"For months I've watched Father age prematurely. He's a lonely person. Both Carl and I had high hopes that would change as he and Laimi became better acquainted. Now that relationship has brought him more pain and sorrow."

"What are you trying to say, Ashley?" Amber asked in an anxious voice.

"Is there a chance that, eventually, you and Father could find happiness with each other?" Ashley boldly asked.

The question hit Amber like a physical blow, and she was at a loss for words. "I don't know how to answer your pointed question, young lady. I've admired your father's honesty and decency ever since I met him. It's just possible that the accident has caused so much pain and hatred that it would be impossible to cultivate a relationship of trust, love and affection.

"I can't answer your question, dear Ashley, but I admire the fact that you want what is best for your father. I agree with you that he deserves better. It's very possible that I could never overcome the shadow of gloom that completely overshadowed our lives, possibly forever." Amber began to cry. "Thank you for sharing your thoughts with me. I can't talk anymore. I'll keep you posted on your Dad's condition."

Ashley hung up the phone with a shaking hand. What a fool she was to put Amber in such a heart-breaking position.

Amber sat in the waiting room with tears running down her cheeks. She had come to Fort Drum to visit old friends. The days were long for her, and she was looking for ways to fill them. She was constantly asking herself that there had to be more to life than what she was now experiencing. She was forty-four years old and had been blessed with good health. Her interest in early American history had occupied her for years when her marriage was crumbling to pieces. Over the years she had fought to keep it together. Then a terrible accident terminated it and became a powerful reminder of how fragile life really is.

The accident had dominated her life. She could have lived with an ordinary accident, but her husband's perversion had so belittled her and robbed her of self-confidence and self-respect that she might never be able to love another man. He had crippled her emotionally. She used to lay awake night after night examining how she could rise above all of the deception and hatred. Nothing worked for her; however, she was able to accept herself more and more since the accident. Healing began after those times she had met with her counterpart, Jon Burke. They both had drawn comfort knowing that the same kind of pain and rejection was shared.

Up until that evening in the Watertown Hospital waiting room, she had denied that she was attracted to Jon Burke. Maybe Ashley had seen through her attempt to hide her feelings. Amber wiped her eyes and smiled at herself. She had planned to visit old friends at Fort Drum the same time that New England states were sending their National Guards to train. She was unsure how she was going to handle the situation, but her aim was to determine if Jon had any interest in her. She had clearly seen how he and Laimi had something going between them, and she admitted that it hurt.

All kinds of doubts filled her head as she waited for word about Jon's condition. She was afraid that her presence might act as a catalyst to fan the flames of bitterness. Instead of mutual attraction, their presence might trigger feelings of remorse and inadequacy.

She was pondering these things when a doctor entered the room and approached her. "We've completed our evaluation of Captain Burke. He had a perforated stomach which is a tear in the lining of the stomach. We've patched that break and sanitized the body cavity."

"Oh thank you, Doctor. I was with Captain Burke when he collapsed at the Officers' Club. His family is back in Maine. I'll notify them immediately. I'm a friend of the family." Amber stood up to face the doctor.

"You were correct to get him to a hospital as soon as possible. It appears that the perforation has been an issue for some time. He'll be under sedation for the evening, so you should get some rest, ma'am. We'll take good care of him. In the morning he'll be hungry and alert."

"Thank you so much, Doctor. Would you leave word with his nurse that I've contacted the family in Maine?" she asked, pleased with the positive message.

Amber was anxious to call Ashley to convey the good news, but she waited until she was back in the privacy of her hotel room. She called for a cab to take her to the Officers' Club where she could get her Buick. Then she rushed to her hotel room where she had a beautiful view of Lake Ontario.

The phone rang just once before Ashley picked up the receiver.

"Hello, Ashley. This is Amber calling. I just came from the hospital. Your father is in the intensive care unit for the evening, and is doing fine. The surgeon told me that he had a perforated lining in his stomach which can be very painful, and that he should make a complete recovery in a short period of time. His vital signs are all normal, and you should not worry about him. He really needs this period to regain his strength and do a little bit of self-examination. He's been under a lot of stress lately."

"Thank you, Amber, for getting back to me so soon. I'll call Carl. He was getting ready to drive to Watertown."

"Your father will be getting a lot of calls from his men in the battalion as soon as he's strong enough to accept visitors. I'll see him every day and report his progress to you. You should be able to speak to him over the phone shortly. If you and your father agree, I will be glad to bring him home with my Buick. I know it would be a difficult trip for you and Carl to make."

"You've been a dear friend, Amber. Thanks for everything," Ashley replied. "I'm angry at myself for intruding into your private life and ask for your forgiveness."

Amber did not want to revisit the conversation. "Your concern for your father is understandable, and I admire you for loving him the way you do. I'm privileged to be a friend of the family. Have a good night's rest, Ashley. I'll call again tomorrow."

"Good night, Amber. You rest well, too."

The next morning Amber went directly to the main desk of the hospital to inquire about Jon's condition. "I'm a friend of Captain Burke's and would like to visit with him."

The nurse at the station told her that the surgeon would not be in until later in the day. "Captain Burke is in room 14 across the hall and is enjoying a light breakfast right now. His vital signs this morning are all normal. He's worried about his battalion. We've received word that he's to be discharged directly home. Another officer from the Maine National Guard has been given the command."

"Thanks, nurse," Amber said, anxious to see him. Her life as an Army brat had given her a unique vantage point to study the men who served in the Army. It was a brotherhood that united every member regardless of financial or social status. Their ability to act as a team prepared them for any stations in life that required selfless acts. She admired the virtues of duty, loyalty, and devotion to country. Her first impression of Jon was based on her life-long opportunity to observe how those virtues were honored. Jon had fit the mold that made it possible for her to believe him when they first unraveled the heartbreaking truth about the deaths of their spouses.

She saw that Jon had a nice view of the lake. He was lying on the bed turned towards the view. She quietly stood beside the bed and spoke in a calm voice. "It's nice to see you alert, Jon. The nurse told me that you have responded well to the operation."

Jon turned to see Amber. "I must have made a scene at the Officers' Club. How bad was I, Amber?"

"You were a very sick person, and everybody at the Club was concerned for you. They got you into an ambulance in a short time. I've called Ashley to tell her how you're doing. When you're up to it I'm sure she will appreciate a call from her dad."

"I will, Amber. I don't want them to worry needlessly about me. My command has been taken over by an officer from Dover-Foxcroft," Jon told her in a strong voice.

"You know how the Army works. Nobody is indispensable, and that's a good thing. If you agree, I can take you home in my Buick. It's a lot more comfortable than an ambulance."

He thought about her offer. "It's a long ways from here. Carl has the coupe at school."

"Well, whatever you suggest, Jon," she quickly stated. She did not want to force herself upon him. "I'm going to go now so that you can rest. I'll stop by this evening if you want." She was reluctant to ask if her presence was a painful reminder of the death of their spouses. She had already passed that test shortly after she met Jon.

He detected her hesitation, and the answer surprised her. "You're a very caring and generous person, Amber Hopkins. My daughter, Ashley, admires your gracious and unselfish ways. I did not mean to rebuff your offer to take me home. There was a time, shortly after the accident, when I relived the ugly scene every time we met. But you must know that that has passed, and you have become a true friend ever since."

Amber was surprised. She had been thinking the same thing. She quickly asked, "Am I interfering too much in your family affairs? If the answer is yes, then it can be immediately rectified."

Jon smiled at her and held out his hands to her. "I'm going to call Ashley to tell her that you're going to take me home and for Carl to stay in school. Would you please pass the phone to me?"

Amber was speechless and passed him the phone. She left to get a cup of coffee at the nearest station so that he could talk to his daughter in private. She saw a large number of soldiers enter Jon's room and took a seat in the lobby to wait for them to leave. She was filled with joy hearing what Jon had told her. Was it possible for the two of them to have a chance for happiness together? They were still strangers in many ways. Suddenly tears began to collect in her eyes, clouding the vision of the soldiers leaving his room. She dried her eyes and finished her coffee before she re-entered the room.

Jon was sitting up, more alert than before. He had been watching the door for her and held out his arms. She sat on the bed and embraced him. He found his voice before she did. "I know that we need more time, Amber, but it's important for me to know if we have a chance…"

She kissed him as tears ran down into her mouth. "I've prayed for this to happen, Jon. I denied the attraction for a long time. After what we've been through, we deserve a chance for happiness. I know that all of the children will be supportive."

He wiped a tear from her cheek. "Ashley just told me that she would love to welcome you into the Burke fold."

Amber was speechless. She silently thanked God for the chance to make this exceptional man happy. She had been frightened to face the future alone, now... it looked brighter than ever. She was ready to embrace it with Jon at her side...

The End

Other Historical Romance Novels
BY
Clifton LaBree

A Song for Lisa   A Historical Romance

This is the story of a young American woman captured by the Japanese in the Philippines, 1941. Like most prisoners, she was brutalized and sadistically treated with a cruel disregard for human life. Three years later, Lisa and her companions had reached the low point of starvation and abuse .....

Lake of Three Sorrows   A Historical Romance

A warm spiritually uplifting story of courage, commitment, and sacrifice. This is the story of Dale Cooper, a battle-weary American soldier who served in two world wars.

Flickering Flame   (Colonial Series Book One)

A historical novel, about the Cullen family who settled in Portsmouth, New Hampshire, and their participation in events prior to the French and Indian War. Freedom and opportunity were on the march, but it extracted a heavy price. Frontier settlers were ruthlessly killed and butchered by rampaging Indians lead by French officers and Jesuit priests who frequently incited them to greater levels of inhumanity...

Raising the Torch   (Colonial Series Book Two)

A continuation of the saga from Flickering Flame, Colonial Series book one, of the Cullen family in Colonial Portsmouth. This is a moving story of love and sacrifice when a small colony had the audacity to fight for independence from their motherland...

Non-Fiction Books

By

Clifton LaBree

New Hampshire's General John Stark, Live Free or Die: Death Is Not the Greatest of Evils

Publisher - Fading Shadows Imprint

A fresh look at one of America's staunchest defenders of liberty and freedom. John Stark was a courageous New Hampshire citizen-soldier who fought in both, the French and Indian War, and the Revolutionary War. His pursuit of leadership excellence on the battlefield distinguished him as one of the most successful combat commanders of the war, and one of the least appreciated.

His selflessness, modest life style, and devotion to the cause of freedom are an inspiration that time has not diminished. He remains today the embodiment of the frugal, independent, and cantankerous New Hampshire Yankee.

Gentle Warrior, General Oliver Prince Smith, USMC

Published by - Kent State University Press. Kent, Ohio, 2001

The Story of one of the United States Marine Corps best General Officer. His flawless performance in Korea is a story that needed to be told.

About: FADING SHADOWS IMPRINT

Fading Shadows Imprint was established to bring to the public books of historical events and portraits of people enduring tragic circumstances of by-gone days. Hopefully, they will generate a deep appreciation and respect for the exceptionalness of the United States of America, and an appreciation for the sacrifice and selflessness of those who valiantly served for liberty and freedom.

The characters are fictional, but the historical events and dates have been seriously researched and are factually presented. Some books feature incidents during the French and Indian Wars as well as the War for Independence.

World Wars I and II are eras rich in stories that beg to be told. I've tried to pay tribute to the collective courage and heroism, often unheralded, that has defined Americans in every engagement. It was a time when the immortality of dreams and aspirations were defended by the blood of young men and women. There is a beautiful monument and cemetery in a small French village where thousands of white crosses and Stars-of-David are set in perfect alignment, honoring thousands of American soldiers who gave their last full measure. A large granite slab bearing mute witness to their sacrifice has the following words chiseled in stone: TIME WILL NOT DIM THE GLORY OF THEIR DEEDS. Another monument reads: VIRTUE AND COURAGE ARE THEIR OWN MONUMENT AND REWARD. Those simple words define the American soldier from the dark days of the Revolutionary War to the present. They are an American treasure, unique in the history of the world.

Every generation has its own signature and characteristics that uniquely define them. The World War II generation is defined by the immortality of the ideals and truth they gallantly defended.

The United States has freely given precious blood and treasure to defend the rights of man to be free, and we have never asked for anything in return. No other nation on the planet has sacrificed so much for the noble virtues of liberty and freedom. We hope that the selections offered by Fading Shadows Imprint will touch your hearts and generate a deeper appreciation and love for our country.

www.ingramcontent.com/pod-product-compliance
Lightning Source LLC
Chambersburg PA
CBHW072126170626
46813CB00004B/1718